NOT MY LOVE STORY

A Movie Magic Novella

DANI MCLEAN

NOT MY LOVE STORY

Book 2 of The Movie Magic Novella series

Copyright © 2022 by Dani McLean

First edition: January 2023

www.danimclean.com

Cover Design by Ink & Laurel

Edited by Beth Lawson at VB Edits

Author photo by Rachael Munro Photography

Also by Dani McLean

The Movie Magic Novella Series:

Midnight, Repeated

Not My Love Story

A Missing Connection - Out Mar 2023

It Has To Be You - Out May 2023

The Forces of Love - Out July 2023

***

The Cocktail Series:

Love & Rum

Sex & Sours

Risks & Whiskey

For anyone who has had to defend their love of romance or any other interest that other people have deemed 'not cool'. Your interests are valid and so are you. People and romance come in all different shapes and sizes. Like what you like, read whatever you want, and be whoever you want to be, wonderful and unashamed!

Authors Note

The Movie Magic Novella series takes place in the fictional location of Chance city.

Chance is a place where anything can (and frequently does) happen. Characters don't always treat these situations as common place, nor do they find them overwhelmingly strange.

Like your favourite movie rom-coms, the magic and wonder of these stories are never explained. Believe anything you want, as long as it makes you happy.

It is a world of wonder, where anything is possible.

Like a fairytale.

Or a beautiful love story.

Harrison
KYLE

Hayley
BENNETT

Not My Love Story

SET THE MOOD PUBLISHING presents "NOT MY LOVE
STORY" a novella by DANI MCLEAN
COVER DESIGN by INK & LAUREL   EDITED by VB EDITS
PRODUCED by COPIOUS AMOUNTS OF CAFFEINE and
ALL THE HALLMARKS

Monday

FADE IN:

1 INT. HOTEL - MEETING ROOM - DAY

Three and half bare beige walls frame a boardroom desk and four chairs. Two men sit opposite each other.

One of them is *not* happy.

———

For Harrison Kyle, the road to misery was lined with rose petals.

"No, Lee. I already told you. I write serious films. Real people, real struggles. I do not write romance." He crossed his arms, grimacing at his soon-to-be ex-best friend. Apparently knowing each other since first grade meant nothing to the asshole, because he was asking Harrison for the one thing he'd promised he wouldn't.

"I'm sorry, buddy. It's too late. I promised the studio, and you owe me."

Lee may have been sorry, but that was hardly a consolation.

Harrison groaned, running a hand through his short hair.

He was boxed in by a completely uninspiring cage. Why was it always beige? His life was a series of color-less rooms — hotels, meeting rooms, studio offices — all attempting to be unique, but only succeeding in matching each other in unoriginality.

He'd flown the red eye for this?

"I've owed you our whole lives," Harrison brushed off. "I'm not doing this."

"It'll get you out of the contract with the studio."

Dammit. If anything would get Harrison to agree to this ridiculous idea, that would be it.

He'd signed the standard non-compete clause when the studio had locked him in to a five-picture deal. He had been too high off the buzz of Sundance to realize that he was signing away his autonomy.

Six years… That's how long he'd been writing other people's ideas. Whatever the studio wanted. Whatever would sell. He missed writing the stories that took shape and evolved in his mind. Ached for it.

And he was so close. One last script, and he'd be free.

"Fine," Harrison said, shucking his sweatshirt and throwing it over the back of his chair. His T-shirt stuck to his skin, damp with sweat, his shoulders aching from the flight. "But we're not friends anymore."

Lee stood, shrugging on a jacket over his red polo. He looked like he was due at an audition as a golf commentator. "I love you too, man."

This was not how Harrison's week was meant to go.

The love movies sold was a farce. A manipulation. And he'd built his career on truths. Exposing them with dialogue and themes until the unyielding light of a camera forced the audience to look squarely at them and themselves.

How the hell was he supposed to write a romance?

A knock came at the door, and Lee paled.

"There's one more thing," he said around a weak laugh. "Actually, you're gonna laugh."

Harrison doubted it.

"For Christ's sake, Lee, what could be worse than roping me into writing a rom-com?"

Lee swallowed and stuck his hands in his jacket pockets.

"Hello, Harry. What a surprise."

At the rich English lilt, Harrison closed his eyes, plotting Lee's demise in increasingly detailed ways. Poison? Too quick. From the obvious way Lee was biting back a laugh, he deserved something elaborate. Painful.

Hayley Bennett waltzed into his periphery, five feet five of sharp wit and temptation. Harrison kept his eyes on Lee. He wasn't ready.

Her voice was infused with fondness. "Oh, come on, Harry. Don't look so glum. This will be fun."

It wouldn't.

Before Lee could slither out the door like the snake he was, Harrison cornered him, lowering his voice so Hayley wouldn't overhear. "I'm not going to forget this. Thirty years of friendship, and you're leaving me stuck here like this is some damn real life rom-com?"

Lee clapped Harrison on the shoulder, cool as anything. If he wasn't careful, his smile would get stuck that way. "Don't look so worried. It's only a week. What's the worst that could happen?"

"I'll send you a list."

A familiar laugh rang out but was quickly covered with a cough, and Harrison turned. Hayley slid gracefully into a seat, the epitome of elegance, her shoulder-length hair carefully tucked behind one ear.

Lee patted Harrison's chest, smug smile firmly in place. Definitely ex-best friend. "You'll be fine."

———

Harrison rolled his battered suitcase into the corner of the room. He'd practically been shoved onto the last-minute flight by the studio, which meant this project was important. He still didn't like it.

Hated even more that he couldn't check in to his room for another few hours, and all he wanted was a decent coffee and a nap.

It didn't help that he was stuck in this tiny bland room, the only sign of life being the glass door and the view beyond it, which was — you guessed it — a beige hallway.

Maybe he could set his next screenplay in a cubicle farm, some sort of pseudo surreal world of endless beige that served as a commentary of how much routine we embraced before it stripped the very color from our lives.

The knot in his stomach tightened. He'd be calmer if he wasn't sardined in this room with the one person he'd spent months avoiding.

Seeing Hayley again was short-circuiting his brain. He'd foolishly hoped he could forget her after the party, but he hadn't counted on Lee selling him out.

Maybe no amount of time would be enough. Six

months hadn't dulled her memory or the impact of seeing her again.

Hayley was just as beautiful as ever, holding court over his senses, and he was a mere jester.

She was smooth to his scruff, always polished and proper. If she'd traveled recently, it didn't show. Where Harrison looked like a mutt rescued from a house fire in a dark T-shirt and loose jeans (the only thing about him that was relaxed), Hayley stunned in crisp, clean tailoring.

Cheekbones, neck, shoulder — her body was a series of alcoves he wanted to hide away in. Her long legs were currently hidden under trousers, leaving only a flash of bare ankle on show. He remembered exactly what her legs felt like wrapped around him and wanted to run his thumb over that delicate skin, dip his fingers lightly under the hem of her pants to see if the same flame sparked to life in her eyes.

Amber, he remembered. A deep, magnetic amber.

"I want to make it clear that I'm only doing this because I'm contracted to." He rifled through his bag for his ear buds. He fucking longed to take a shower, to wash off the stale smell of recycled plane air and his frustrations.

"Don't worry. It's exceedingly obvious that you don't want to be here. And since you couldn't find love if you fell into a vat of it, I don't expect that you'll be any help."

Well, at least her expectations were reasonable.

"I'll take that as a compliment since these films are all the same. Vapid and uninspired."

"You're calling my work vapid?"

He shrugged, the lie twisting in his gut. Truthfully, her writing was insightful, though crippled by the idiotic conventions she played to. But there was no denying her talent, nor her success. Her last movie had outsold his by an entire decimal point, even if her name had been buried in the credits.

He wasn't sure what pissed him off more.

Lee had made it clear that the studio wanted him here because of the acclaim his films had always achieved (he'd take the Academy's accolades over what appealed to the average person). But if they had hoped he could raise this drivel to his usual heights, they were mistaken.

Hayley didn't need help. And he didn't want to be here. It should be a no-brainer.

But if suffering through this week meant he could make his own stuff again, he'd take it.

"There are only so many ways you can write city girl meets boy from the other side of the tracks before it loses all meaning."

Hayley barked out a short laugh. "Oh, and I suppose those long, moody films about the destruction of hope in a cold world are all completely distinguish-able from each other."

"At least they don't sugarcoat reality."

"No, they just make me want to cry in the shower."

Great. Now all he could think about was her, clothes and all, wet and dripping.

He cleared his throat. That *wasn't* helping. "But they make you feel something."

Hayley tapped her pen, frowning. "You might have buried your heart in concrete at the bottom of a very deep ocean, but romance makes the rest of humanity feel things, too."

Oh, he knew all about the lies romance told — the fantasy of a partner who was perfect, illusions of relationships that never faced hardship or needed work. In romance movies, the hard part was saying I love you, not what happened after the credits rolled.

That was where the real stories began.

"Please. They're all the same. Paint-by-numbers plots with catchy posters. They're nothing but money catchers with no substance." Probably a low blow, but in for a penny and all that. "Is she a young girl trying to make it in the big city? She'll be on the poster in a red outfit. Generic rom-com featuring Hollywood's buff flavor of the month? The couple standing back to back on a white background."

"Oh, hell," she said, searching in the pockets of her suede jacket, piling the retrieved items onto the table in front of her. A room key, a hair elastic, and a collection of empty sugar packets. Her refined posture already showed cracks. *He was getting to her.* "Are you going to be like this the entire week?"

"And another thing," he continued.

"Oh good. I was hoping you weren't finished," she drawled.

"Half the time, the couple falls in love way too fast. Instant love. Mix a handful of outdated jokes about gender with whatever top 40 songs will quickly date your movie and bam! Holiday hit."

"Be more of a stereotype, I beg of you," Hayley muttered, staring into the distance.

"You can't honestly make me believe two people are made for each other in a week."

Hayley moved, covering the distance between them in short, unhurried steps. She placed her hands on either side of him and leaned in. God, he'd barely need to move to kiss her. Jasmine and sugar swarmed him, the heat of her body a beacon. His nerve endings lit with the memory of the last time they were this close. And closer.

"Oh, I can and I will."

For a long breath, he said nothing, too caught up in *her*. He couldn't believe he'd agreed to this.

"I have one rule," he said.

She waited. Had her lashes always been so long?

"You even breathe the words *Love Actually*, and I'm out of here."

Her laugh was summer rain, welcome and soothing, and far too pure for his iced-over heart.

"Deal."

———

Their differences were even more obvious when they unpacked, as though Harrison needed a reminder that he wasn't from her world and never would be.

He reached for his backpack and pulled out his Post-its and array of pens, arranging them neatly on the table and leaving his laptop in his bag. Harrison approached outlining hands-on, needing to see the shape of the narrative take place before him. He could never see the beginning until he'd imagined the end. Mapping out how to get between those points was the fun part.

And this way, he could color coordinate.

From her case, Hayley retrieved a notebook, a single blue pen, more empty sugar packets (which she frowned prettily at), and her laptop, which she placed beside her.

When she was done, he sighed. "Let's get this over with."

Her gaze slid across to him, as powerful as a caress, and his gut clenched.

One week. That was all he needed to get through.

———

The longest wall in the room acted as their planning board. Yellow Post-its denoted the acts, green the major plot beats, blue the emotional ones.

Typically, this was where Harrison would get to work.

They just had one itty, bitty problem.

Hayley stared across the table. "You honestly can't name a single romance you've enjoyed?"

"No." How many times did he need to say it?

"What about those raunch-coms that are all about sex and weed and blue humor?"

"Please tell me you think more of me than that." Those films had about as much to do with romance as Harrison did with a pro-surfer — neither had a shred of evidence to back them up. "They're funny, but they aren't romance."

"Says the self-proclaimed enemy of romance movies."

"You're saying I should hate something I know nothing about?"

A deep groan left her throat while she pinched her nose. The way it crinkled in annoyance was cute. He'd missed it.

"I'd almost forgotten you were like this."

Frustration was a damn good look on her.

He cocked a grin, unable to resist teasing her. "Irresistible?"

"Impossible." A flicker of amusement crossed her face, and his pulse spiked.

He smoothed his smile into something genuine. It was damn good to know he could still get under her skin.

"Come on, Harry. You've never seen a script you didn't have an opinion on. Give me one idea."

Fine. "Unfairly attractive twentysomething girl meets unfairly attractive twentysomething guy. Probably in a coffee shop. One of them spills something or there's a mix-up of some sort. Bonus points if she's from out of town and he's in a suit."

Across from him, Hayley was seething, her silver pen tap-tap-tapping on the blank page. It probably shouldn't turn him on, but when she got this angry, she took to chewing on the corner of her lip, leaving it red and distracting.

"You're trying very hard to make me dislike you," she said. Her accent curled around the words, a flame to his kindling.

"While you are a delight." He winked.

She stood, studying their progress on the board with her back to him. In the silence he took her in, the way her crossed arms pulled her shirt across her back, the dip of her spine, the curve of her hips.

He adjusted himself, hiding his body's traitorous reaction.

When she turned to look at him over her shoulder, he knew he'd been caught.

"Something on your mind, Harry?" Hayley asked, and all he could hear was her moaning his name.

There was a hell of a lot on his mind, none of it PG or remotely professional.

The room shrunk, too small to hold them both along with the elephant they were ignoring.

This week was going to be slow torture.

"This is awful," he said finally.

Hayley ignored his whining, which was probably for the best. One of them had to be an adult. She stuck a note to the wall, marked *one bed?*. "And yet you're still here."

He sank farther into the cheap office chair. "Not by choice."

She arched one perfectly curved brow. "I don't buy that for a second. *Again, With Feeling* was a critical darling. If you truly didn't want to be here, you wouldn't be."

Pride swamped him, mixed with surprise. His name hadn't been attached to that film. Not publicly, anyway.

He was the third screenwriter they'd brought in. He'd torn the original to pieces and built it back up until it barely resembled the garbage fire it had started as. But the studio had needed a vehicle for their favorite director, and after a few lines were altered, the screenwriting credit had gone to him. Whatever. Harrison was only *mostly* bitter about it. "How did you know it was mine?"

"The scene by the river, where she's talking to her father. She says, 'I wish you'd known how to love me. I never learned how.' There's something quietly poignant about your stories. The main character is always searching for something. Resolution. Retribution. What happens when they find it?"

"That's usually called the end."

Her eyes sparkled. "Sounds very similar to a happily ever after."

He'd known that was coming, even as the words left his mouth.

"You're enjoying this, aren't you?"

"A little. You're cute when you admit I'm right."

Against his better judgment, he laughed. "You'll have to wait a little longer to hear that."

"Look. We have a week to deliver this. How long do you plan on sulking?"

He leaned back, crossing his arms over his chest. "Seven days should do it."

She raised her gaze to the ceiling, lips pursed. No doubt cursing him.

"If you're sincerely dedicated to being as unhelpful as possible, why don't you sit quietly while I work?"

Now *that* they could agree on.

Harrison was about to beat level 7573 when an elegant hand firmly placed a twenty-dollar bill in front of him. Five perfectly manicured nails tapped the table, short and clear, and he held back a smile while he made Hayley wait, finishing his level before slipping one earbud out and turning to her.

"Can I help you?"

The tapping stopped. Her eyes glittered, even under the horrendous fluorescents. They were captivating at any distance but were especially dangerous to Harrison's control up close.

"There's a coffee shop on the corner. I'd like an Earl Grey. A splash of milk, no sugar."

"You want to pay six dollars for hot water and a tea bag?"

"With a dash of milk."

He was halfway to the door when she added, "Oh, and maybe you can buy yourself a sunny disposition while you're out."

"Sorry, last time I checked, they were sold out."

Her eye roll was the last thing he saw as he stepped into the hall.

6 INT COFFEE SHOP — DAY

    Harrison waits in line. The coffee shop is crowded with young, attractive people, every available surface covered in Valentine's Day paraphernalia.

———

I t was busier than he expected.

Every seat was taken, and what looked like a first date was happening in the far corner. The young woman played with her hair while he inched his hand toward hers on the table, landing the punchline of a joke that sent her into a fit of giggles.

Hayley couldn't have written it better.

Was this whole city drunk on love?

Something small hit his calf, and when he looked down, a cell phone lay at his feet, mercifully unbroken. As he reached for it, a gentle hand collided with his.

Behind him stood a very pretty blonde in a sundress. The dress was an odd choice, considering it was still winter, but Harrison knew better than to judge anyone's fashion choices when he regularly exemplified the term *haphazard*.

"Hi there," she said, collecting the phone. "I'm Beth. Sorry about that. I'm so clumsy today. Or nervous, but nerves always make me clumsy."

He nodded, taking a step forward as the line moved.

"Are you here for the festival?"

He didn't want to talk. He thought he'd been broad-casting that clearly enough with his back turned, but she plowed ahead. Fitting, considering her thick southern accent was forcing images of hay bales and tractors into his mind.

"I didn't even know there was such a thing as a Valentine's festival. Imagine my surprise when I heard about it!"

He could imagine. Wasn't the ridiculous holiday enough of an overblown spectacle?

Capitalism had a lot to answer for.

"I only just arrived this morning."

Oh good, she wasn't done.

"I was supposed to be with my best friend — she makes the most amazing chocolates, and she's a finalist in the hearts and kisses competition — but she couldn't make it, so I agreed to come in her place." She brushed her hand along his forearm, leaning in to whisper loudly, "Don't tell anyone. I've already met one of the judges, and he's been so rude already."

Harrison couldn't help it. He laughed. Had Hayley sent a friend to give him this ridiculous story as payback?

But Beth's face crumpled at the sound. *Shit.* It was one thing to trade barbs with Hayley; she was strong and sharp and deadly. Beth looked like every bright-eyed ingenue in a made-for-TV movie.

Christ, he was a dick.

"Don't worry. Your secret's safe with me."

The smile leapt back in place, and the line before him blessedly cleared.

He quickly stepped forward. "Earl Grey and an espresso. Oh, and I'll get hers as well." He threw some extra cash on the counter.

Beth practically swooned. "Aw, that's so sweet of you."

He shrugged. Yes, she was overly optimistic, and he was certain her heart would be crushed someday, but he couldn't let himself be the reason she realized life was disappointing. No doubt the city would wring out the sparkle in her eyes… and didn't that thought kick him in the nuts?

———

The coffee shop gave Harrison the creeps. Now that he'd had enough time to take the place in, with its too-cheerful staff and little hanging plants, he couldn't shake the strange feeling it gave him. The whole scene could have been lifted straight from a TV show about singles in the city.

It'd probably be perfect for the film. *Busy professionals crossing paths at their regular morning stop. A mix-up and swapping of numbers later…*

He stopped himself. How annoyingly bland. No doubt Hayley would love it.

While he waited, Harrison contented himself with pocketing half a dozen sugar packets, the same he'd seen her with earlier. He wasn't sure why anyone would even bother with tea, but if she wanted to drink a cup of hot sweet milk, who was he to care?

Hayley was exactly as he remembered. Too observant, too tempting. He'd hoped sleeping together would be enough to satisfy his interest, scratch that ever-present itch to know everything about her, see her in every light, explore every inch of her mind.

That line of thinking could only lead to getting hurt, so Harrison had made do with exploring her body instead.

And what a fucking body.

It hadn't been enough. He'd known it wouldn't be, but he'd never been good at staying away.

He caught the eye of the barista over the counter. Tall, lean, dimples. The man was cute, in a doe-eyed, optimistic, kind of way. Definitely interested.

And maybe a few years ago, Harrison would have pursued it, but it always ended the same. A couple of hot and eager blowjobs, and then his attitude would send them running.

It was how all his relationships ended. No candle-light dinners, no walks on the beach. Just a quick lay, and a fast exit.

He carefully avoided eye contact when his order was called, checking the names scrawled on the cups, avoiding one with *Kelly* written in messy script. When his first sip was not the black coffee he'd ordered but an overly sweet hazelnut monstrosity, he grimaced.

Hayley's Earl Grey mocked him from the counter.

"Oh." A tall brunette giggled, appearing out of nowhere. Was laughing gas being pumped into the air of the shop this morning? "I think they mixed up our drinks. I'm Kelly. Obviously. And this extremely black coffee must be yours." She held it out to him, and they swapped. "Do you have something against milk and sugar, or are you sweet enough as you are?"

"No one has ever accused me of being sweet before."

"Maybe they don't see the real you," she said, giving him a once-over.

Harrison was not usually opposed to a little flirtation, even in a strange little shop on a Monday morning, but this was the second time in twenty minutes a woman had come on to him, and even his ego wasn't big enough to explain that.

As he turned to leave, Kelly put her hand on his forearm, halting him and pulling a pen out of her pocket.

"Here." She plucked the cup from his hand and wrote her phone number just below her name. "In case you get a sweet tooth later."

What the hell was happening today?

———

He couldn't even make it out of the coffee shop.

The collision was inescapable, considering how his day had gone so far. Espresso soaked the front of his shirt. Shock set in quickly, until he realized he wasn't burned.

Something very strange was going on.

"I'm so sorry."

Harrison looked up. He had no words.

This time it was a redhead.

What next?

The man before him dabbed at the stain, a wad of napkins captured in a strong hand.

Harrison followed the arm, taking in the rest of him. Gray slacks, matching vest, stark white shirt. The same interested glint as Beth and Kelly and the barista.

Was this all a delirious hallucination? Had he suffered a brain injury after Lee had broken the bad news, and now he was imagining himself trapped in a damn rom-com?

Meet-cutes weren't real.

"That looks like it's going to stain. I'd be happy to take if off you if you want — back at my place. Help you wash it." The man's jaw could cut glass. "Unless you prefer being dirty." He cocked a brow and gave Harrison a pointed look.

Harrison looked down at himself, confused. Of course, Hayley's Earl Grey was unharmed. He wanted to laugh.

He needed to get out of this damn shop before another lovesick stranger came on to him.

"Sorry, I have to be somewhere… else."

———

Lee picked up on the second ring. "What —"

"Did you do this?"

"Do what?"

"Six years, Lee —"

"I know."

"And *Marked* is still sitting in development hell —"

"I *know.*"

"I was supposed to be done by now."

"Kyle, man, I know. Why do you think you're here? This is your ticket out."

"God dammit…"

It had to be some sort of cosmic joke. Harrison had been asking Lee to find him a way to finish up with the studio for months. He couldn't turn this down. No matter how much he hated romance.

And Lee knew it.

Harrison groaned, running a hand down his face. He needed a shave. "All right, stop looking so smug." It didn't matter that he couldn't see him; he knew Lee. "Go putt a birdie or whatever it is you spend my money on. But I swear, if you're behind this, you aren't nearly as funny as you think you are."

Lee only laughed. "No idea what you're talking about, man."

———

Hayley couldn't quite hide her smile upon seeing him, although she tried, covering her mouth with one hand. "What happened to you?"

The explanation sounded twice as ridiculous as he expected it to, and Hayley was predictably moved to tears. Of laughter. The sound filled the room, and Harrison ignored the way it filled him up as well.

A week of this, and he'd be back to his own screenplays. He needed to stay focused on that.

"I hate to say it," she said, her eyes alight and her cheeks pink. She was a vision.

"Yeah, you look like you hate it."

"For someone so determined to look down on romance, I'd say your good fortune is well deserved. Almost, dare I say, karmic?"

"Very funny. Maybe you should reconsider your day job. You may have a future in stand-up comedy."

She laughed, adding three packets of sugar to her milky tea. It wasn't the first time he'd witnessed this ritual. Always three, no more, no less, and always personally added, as if she didn't trust the barista to count properly.

It was endearing. Harrison was used to being the tightly wound, nit-picky cynic with an attention to detail that somehow got lost on his way to dressing himself. Messy on the outside and ordered on the inside was what his sister always said.

He could learn a thing or two from Hayley. Hell, she'd likely jump at the chance to teach him, and *shit* he really shouldn't have put that particular scene in his head. Now he'd have to sit here and not let his dick take over the thinking every time she chewed on the end of her ballpoint.

He was such an asshole.

He stood.

"I'm going to go check in."

Hayley nodded over her tea, her eyes polished bronze. He grabbed his stuff, his traitorous heart rattling the bars of its cage as he walked out of the room.

11 INT. HOTEL — RECEPTION DESK

The hotel manager enters his
details while Harrison waits.

———

The lobby was quite nice for a mid-budget hotel. The vaulted ceiling spilled light into the room, bringing to life the flecks of golden brown in the terrazzo flooring that only dragged Harrison's mind back to the woman he'd walked away from.

Again.

"Mr. Kyle, I'm so sorry, but there's been a mix-up with your room."

Harrison's exhale was dragged from the depths of his feet. All he wanted was for this day to end, but it seemed determined to throw everything it could at him.

"Please tell me you're joking. I'm running on two hours of sleep and three terrible coffees, one of which I'm wearing. All I want is to shower and change. So if you're about to tell me that I flew all the way here and I don't have a room, I'm going to need you to not do that."

"No, no! Nothing like that. You definitely have a room. It's… just…"

"What?" How could this get worse?

"Well, you see, the thing is," he said, tapping away at the computer, "we're completely booked up with the Valentine's festival, and we've had a few double book-

ings, so we've had to move you from where we'd origi-
nally had you placed. No extra charge, of course."

The festival. Of course. How could he forget?

Harrison braced himself. "Tell me."

"It's the honeymoon suite."

Harrison's laugh reverberated off the high ceilings.
He was cursed. Had to be.

"Sure, okay. Why not?"

The manager looked relieved. Harrison kind of
wanted to scream. Hayley would probably tell him to
untwist his knickers, and she'd be right. But dammit,
today was veering into independently distributed terri-
tory. If one more absurd thing happened, he would turn
this wacky comedy of errors into a court drama. And he
was not the kind of protagonist audiences would look
favorably on.

He was far more anti than hero, thank you very
much.

Once the keycard was handed over, all Harrison
could focus on was locking himself away and forgetting
that today had even happened.

He didn't want to like the suite, but it was nice.
Though the beige reckoning persisted — walls, ceiling,
carefully selected abstract paintings that Harrison was
sure were bought in bulk from an overseas printing
factory — it clearly paid to be in the best room of the
house.

He even liked the pops of gold, rich timber furni-
ture, and drapings of deep green, moody and seductive,
which ran throughout. Crisp white flooded the bathroom, with its claw foot tub and double sink.

The single bedroom looked out over the river, with city views continuing from the separate lounge. There was even a damn breakfast nook, stocked full of teas and coffees. No Earl Grey, though.

Harrison slunk around every corner, checking for petals and champagne. Now he was being ridiculous. When he found none, he finally slumped into the bed and toed off his shoes.

Lee really had a lot to answer for. The only way this could get worse was if he'd been stuck here with Hayley. God help him.

He dialed the familiar number and couldn't remember the last time they'd talked this regularly.

"Lee, I swear to god if you are behind this, I'm going to murder you. And enjoy it."

"So violent today," he said. "Hayley's really getting to you, huh?"

"I can handle Hayley."

"Mm-hmm. So you've mentioned."

"Are seriously telling me you had nothing to do with this?"

"I solemnly promise I have nothing to apologize for."

Harrison believed him, but Lee didn't have to sound so damn pleased about it. He wasn't the one wearing his coffee.

"It's gotta be her, then. If she thinks I'm going to lie down and take it, then she has severely underestimated me."

"It's like sixth grade all over again. You were obsessed with —"

"I wasn't obsessed," Harrison argued.

"Bullshit. Hey, here's a thought. Maybe don't antagonize your cowriter. You're a big boy now. Suck it up, finish the script — hell, let her do all the work, and by the end of the week, you'll be free."

But the thought of his name being attached to a project and not at least attempting to make it something he could be proud of was worse than walking back into that damn coffee shop. No, he was going to do everything he could to make sure this wouldn't end up the black mark on his career. He had a reputation to uphold.

And even Hayley Bennett, with her biteable lips and perfect skin, wasn't going to mess with that.

———

After a long shower and two fingers of whiskey he planned on charging to Lee (the bastard), Harrison threw on a robe, relaxed on the sofa, and went in search of one of Hayley's films.

It was as trite and cliché as he remembered, but there, within the seams, between the chalkboard outlines of the so-called characters, was Hayley's warmth, wit, and heart.

And dammit, he wanted more.

He was going to actually do this, wasn't he?

The grimace rumbled through his bones. A *rom-com*. *Fuck*.

Tuesday

A ny hope of a quiet, unassuming morning was swiftly dashed when the elevator doors opened to reveal the hotel manager and his oddly knowing smile. Pre-caffeine Harrison wasn't his best look, and even the calm of an unhurried jerk hadn't improved his mood this morning.

"Morning, Mr. Kyle. Which floor?"

"Ground," he mumbled.

"Going to visit our breakfast buffet, or taking yourself to enjoy a meal at one of the excellent cafés nearby? If you need a recommendation, I'd be happy to assist."

Jesus *Christ*. There should be a law against being this energetic. Maybe his pep was a little more chemical than Harrison had first assumed.

He could use some chemical encouragement. Preferably in a mug with infinite refills.

"I'm fine."

"We wanted to apologize for the room mix-up yesterday. As a gesture, I have this." He then presented Harrison with a stuffed bear the size of a toddler. Where the hell had he been hiding that thing?

Emblazoned across its chest was a glittering red heart and the words "Be My Valentine." Overhead, a pop song warbled about a beach house.

Harrison scratched the scruff on his jaw. "Ah…"

What — and he couldn't stress this enough — the actual fuck?

———

Hayley was already seated in the hotel restaurant when he arrived, tea cup and notepad on the table. Sliding into the chair across from her, Harrison wasn't prepared for the way her eyes brightened.

"Good morning, Harry. Who's your friend?"

Dammit, he loved the way his name sounded on her lips. The 'H' was softer, rounded. Smooth. Like an aged red.

He tucked the bear under the table. "Uh, no one."

"Not a morning person, I see," she said, the curl of her mouth rising sweetly.

"Oh, hello. Excuse me," Hayley waved down a passing server. "My friend here needs coffee. Rather a lot of it."

The young girl blushed. Hayley often had that effect on people. "Sure, I'll be right back."

Any hope that he'd find Hayley completely unappealing was a lost cause, as it always was.

Her hair was down, brown waves flipped to the side, the way it always ended up while she was deep in thought. Hungrily, he followed the drape of her sweater off a single shoulder, his eyes drawn to where it exposed hundreds of tiny freckles. They hadn't had the chance to undress last time, and it was a damn shame.

"Thank you," he said, for more than the coffee.

Hayley had raised her tea, her long lashes sweeping up to pin him with the same clever eyes that were his undoing. "You're welcome."

He found himself entranced by the steady movement of her fingers, the graceful tilt of her head, as she worked, making notes in the same worn notebook he'd seen her with yesterday.

He desperately wanted to know what it was filled with.

When the server returned with his coffee, he practically moaned.

"Don't you find it annoying to write everything down?" he asked, his brain firing up. "You'll just have to type it up later. It's a waste."

She laid the pen down and arched a brow at him. "I don't like having my laptop at the table. It feels rude. This way I can make notes while I eat. It helps me tease out all the ideas I may have had during the night."

Vivid memories of a night when she'd had some very good ideas surfaced then, even though he'd made a silent promise to stop jumping to those thoughts. *One week*, he reminded himself.

He nodded toward the buffet. "I'm gonna grab breakfast. Can I get you anything?"

"No, thank you."

It was as expected: powdered eggs, dry bacon, greasy potatoes, a selection of cereals, fruits, and yogurt. He loaded two plates: one hot, one cold.

"You either have a very high metabolism, or you're secretly a hobbit," Hayley teased when he returned.

Another green tick checked off in his brain, especially gleeful at the reference. He'd devoured those books as a kid.

"Before I forget," he said, handing over the dozen sugar packets he'd pocketed from the buffet.

Then he focused on his food.

There was no way he was steady enough for the full weight of Hayley's attention. Not without potentially embarrassing himself. The chances were high when she was involved.

But as the silence dragged on and his mind woke up, it was difficult to ignore his guilt. It wasn't her fault he preferred to work alone and so was terrible at partnering and peopling in general. The least he could do was apologize.

"Look. I'm sorry about how I acted yesterday. I know it's not your fault that I'm here. I shouldn't have taken it out on you."

Across the table, she pressed her lips together, then relaxed, working around something she wasn't saying. Probably an insult. He deserved it. He might not have wanted this job, but he was a professional, and he wanted her to know he could, and would, get his act together.

"Thank you, Harry. Apology accepted."

He liked Hayley, and she was a talented writer. Maybe the project wasn't as doomed as it had seemed yesterday. Maybe... he might even like working with her.

A tug on his shirt got his attention. Beside him stood a young boy, nervously rocking on his heels, his attention solely on the bear.

"I like your bear."

"Uh, thanks." Harrison picked it up. When life hands you an obscenely large Valentine's gift... "You can have it if you want."

Two wide eyes shot up to meet his. "Really?"

Harrison nodded, and the boy took it and ran off with barely a glance.

Hayley's questioning look sent him staring down at his coffee.

"What? I'm too old for toys."

"I don't know. Something tells me there's a heart under all that cynicism."

He shrugged. "That's indigestion."

Her pale neck lengthened when she tilted her head back and laughed. It was a great sound. Considering he spent most of his time pissing people off, making Hayley laugh always stirred up his gut something fierce. What could he say? She had a great laugh.

She had a great everything.

———

"Show me what you have so far."

Hayley slid her laptop over to him, leaning in close. Heat cascaded from her and seeped into his shoulder, making it difficult to concentrate.

The plot wasn't bad, if a little predictable. Rivals with differing work styles forced to work together... a little on the nose. But yesterday he'd been thinking about cubicle farms, so who was he to judge? "It's..."

"You're about to be horrible, aren't you?"

"I was actually going to say it's brilliant."

"Really," she said dryly.

Clearly, it would take a lot more to fool her. He

sighed. "Okay, I'll be honest. It's not revolutionary. Not terrible; just a little… predictable."

"Here we go." She moved around the table, taking her laptop and all of Harrison's attention. "I suppose you're used to something flashier, like cerulean."

"Obsidian is more my color."

She broke out in a laugh, then rolled up the sleeves of her shirt and turned to him. "So tell me, oh wise one. How can we improve it?"

We. Nope, couldn't think about that. "Your protag has some potential, and I don't hate the idea of them being opposites. Instead of rivals, why not make them work together? She's a designer, right? And her goal is to sell the uh, the whatever it is, to the big conglomerate wholesaler?" Pro tip for mass market movies — the details hardly mattered. Whatever the MacGuffin was could be dealt with in rewrites.

Hayley nodded.

"So maybe he's a marketing consultant. He's brought in because while she knows the technical side, he knows exactly how to sell it."

"Working together for a common goal is a great start." Sometimes when she smiled, it would curl up deeper on one side of her face. He could lose hours to that little dip in her cheek.

"Exactly. They can still disagree, but this way, I don't have to believe two people who dislike each other would do a total one-eighty in a matter of days."

"You're certainly well versed in romance tropes for someone who hates them so much."

"I need to know what to avoid."

Her laughter was lyrical. "Sure, let's pretend that's true."

Harrison huffed a laugh.

Hayley beamed and sat a little straighter. "Put your posturing aside for one second and live a little. You might even enjoy yourself."

That's what he was worried about.

———

Unsurprisingly — and to Harrison's great relief — Hayley took over working on the plot, easily batting away his increasingly sarcastic suggestions. Watching her work was fascinating and arousing in turn, and she'd even taken his complaints into consideration and mapped out an outline that he didn't hate.

Beside him, his phone rattled. He smiled at his sister's text.

Emilia: Warner broke your high score

> **H**: That sneak! I told him no practicing while I was gone. How'd group go?

Emilia: Surprisingly well. Casey finally opened up. Not much, but it was great progress. I'm proud of her.

> **H**: I'm proud of you

Emilia: Sap. How's Hayley?

Quickly, he checked that his screen couldn't be seen. Across the table, Hayley balled up a sugar packet and flicked it with her nail into a nearby wastebasket. Every time she made it, she made this little sound of elation. He'd started to grind his teeth together to stop himself from smiling. His jaw had been aching for the last hour.

H: Subtle. Could go either way. She hasn't killed me yet.

Emilia: Now I'm really shocked. Pull your finger out already.

H: Stop trying to be cool. You're too old for that. And tell Warner I'm gonna get him back for that high score.

Emilia: You deserve happiness!! One of these days, you're going to believe me.

Another packet shot across the table, bouncing off the rim before falling into the goal.

Eventually, he had to know.

"Why do you write these?"

It didn't fit with anything else he knew about her. Clever and quick-witted, she'd attended some prestigious school in the UK before moving continents. Surely, she saw how reductive these stories were, didn't she?

"Because I enjoy them. Haven't you ever met someone and felt an indescribable chemistry? And the more you get to know them, the more you want to know, and the more you want to share, until you can't imagine your life without them?"

Suddenly, the table became extremely fascinating to him.

She continued. "I love trying to capture that first spark. Where two people are living their lives, unaware, and then suddenly…"

"Magic," he finished, somehow knowing exactly what she was going to say.

He lifted his gaze, thunderstruck by the open expression she wore. Those wide eyes and the breathtaking smile. When had he last been that unguarded?

"And you don't mind that it isn't real?"

"Isn't that all the more reason to write it? If it isn't possible, as you say, then why not write the impossible? Experience it, if just for a moment."

It was hard to remember when faced head-on with her enthusiasm.

"I know my stories aren't always reflective of real life, but why can't they be? Why don't we strive to make reality more like a romance? Embrace the possibility of love at every moment? Why not let hope drive us and motivate us to find something truly meaningful?"

Put that way, it made him wish it was real. Maybe not for himself; that seemed like tempting fate. But for her.

For Emilia.

———

Of course, no good thing could last where Harrison was concerned.

Honestly, he'd never known when to keep his mouth

shut. And getting a reaction from Hayley was infinitely more fun than thinking about meet-cutes.

This was why he preferred working alone.

Hayley looked like she wanted to skewer him with her pen. Harrison almost wanted her to. It couldn't be half as painful as fighting over expositional dialogue.

"Harry, please," she pleaded.

"Too much?"

She pinched the bridge of her nose. "Have you seen *John Wick*?"

He nodded. Who hadn't?

"Well. If you keep talking, I'm going to follow his example and destroy you with this pen. Not just once. But many, many times. And I'm going to enjoy it."

"If you really want to stick me with something, you only need to ask."

"Stop distracting me."

He wished he could.

Truth was, he'd never had any self-control when it came to her. Even during the months he'd enforced his own ban on pursuing her, he'd followed her career closely, trying not to feel like the world's biggest creep by reliving their night together.

No, the best thing he could do was remind her of what a terrible combination they were. Oil and water. Toothpaste and orange juice. Jared Leto and the Joker.

There wasn't any way of putting distance between them, not in a room this small, but that didn't stop him from trying.

A weary sigh preceded her next question. "Why do

you hate these movies so much? You're practically waging a one-man war against love."

"Bit melodramatic, don't you think?" he said, avoiding his reasons to focus on their Post-it wall, the pops of color breaking up the beige.

In all the years that they'd crossed paths, events and film festivals and social gatherings, he'd been drawn to her. And every single time, he had put himself in her path, soaking in the familiar crackle of wit and intrigue around her, hypnotized by the fire in her eyes.

When she focused on him, the room disappeared. No one existed except the two of them.

He couldn't get enough.

It's why he'd stayed away. The industry was abysmally small, giving him multiple chances to see her again, and he'd avoided every single one.

But now that he was back in her orbit, he wondered how he'd managed to be without it.

How had he gone a single day without her smile, or her sharp focus and rapier tongue, as talented with words as it was stroking his own? Trailing the rivets of his abs, or the throbbing vein along his cock.

Fuck. *Don't think about that.*

When he looked over at her, Hayley simply raised her eyebrows, challenging him without a single word.

He relented. "I've never seen a single one I could believe in." It wasn't the full story, but it wasn't a lie.

"And now you have the power to change that. Or are you not up to the challenge?" she teased. "I seem to remember you having more stamina than this."

Now she was playing dirty.

Harrison splayed his legs a little wider, celebrating when her eyes darted down to admire him. He decided to stoke the fire. "Care to test that theory?"

His relief was palpable when she rolled her eyes and turned back to the dialogue they'd been arguing over. Good. He didn't need Hayley and her clever eyes looking too closely. His heart was raw already. And despite what she likely thought, he did have one. Battered and bruised, stuffed in a box in a drawer under a blanket in the basement of his soul, perhaps, but it existed.

Let her keep her image of him as a jaded writer who couldn't see the merit in whispered promises or rose-colored futures. Because the truth — the embarrassing, unavoidable truth — would mean admitting that he'd once bought all of it, every last lie, wanted it, dreamed it, craved it for himself, until he realized how futile the search was.

How easily he could fake those promises in his writing.

And Hayley wondered why he had a problem with romance movies.

———

When Hayley suggested getting tea, he was... well, he wasn't afraid. That would be ridiculous. He was simply... concerned. For the script. Because he hadn't contributed much.

"Whose fault is that?" Hayley mocked.

It had nothing at all to do with a certain coffee shop and his newfound fear of meet-cutes.

"Fine, oh precious one. Would you like me to come with you?"

It was on the tip of his tongue to lob the tease back at her, remembering very clearly the last time they had come together. He wished his body didn't remember it so well, actually. He hadn't been able to picture anything — scratch that, anyone — while coming since.

"You did say you needed some inspiration. And I could use the fresh air. I guess I could go with you if you wanted."

"If I wanted," she drawled.

"See how chivalrous I am?"

He really wished he could bottle that spark inside her. A potent combination of narrowed eyes, one-sided smile, and something undeniably Hayley.

And how was he supposed to resist that?

He was only a man, after all.

———

Small community gardens were hidden all over Chance City, he'd heard, down alleyways and behind office blocks. Walk ten minutes in any direction, and one would appear. It only took a little time and knowing where to look.

Reminders of the upcoming Valentine's festival flashed him at every turn — hearts in windows, pinker than a *Grease* sing-a-long, flowers and chocolates and music.

40

"Isn't it beautiful?" Hayley asked after stopping to watch a group of teenagers posing and taking selfies in front of a mural of rainbow-colored graffiti hearts. "My mother would love this."

He'd seen her at events, parties, premieres — work commitments that had put him in her vicinity — but never long enough to see her like this: private, unguarded.

It was as if someone had turned her happiness up to eleven. She was radiant. What would it be like to harbor so much joy?

Harrison wasn't unfeeling. He liked dating, though he hadn't done it in a while, and he loved sex. But he'd never met anyone who inspired anything incredible in him. The way the movies made people believe they could.

He stuffed his hands into the pockets of his jeans. "Did your parents end up taking that trip to Scotland?"

"No, my mother wasn't able to fly in the end. But her cousin came down after the funeral, brought some of my grandfather's belongings to pass on. They spent a week getting sauced and reminiscing. Called me every day at eleven p.m. with a new story."

"Sounds like a fun time."

Their arms brushed. "Oh, she'd love you. She's always begging me to bring someone home."

"Maybe I'll drop by."

"Maybe you should."

Hayley turned to him, and for a shocking second, he swore his heart had stopped. God, what he wouldn't give to know what love felt like.

Maybe then he could begin to explain what he felt every time she was near him.

———

The courtyard they found was blissfully quiet, even though there were at least two dozen people around. There was a food cart set up in the corner, selling chori-pan, and a couple snuggled together, whispering. The cold sting of February hung in the air, even as the build-ings shield them from the wind.

Taking the last empty bench he could find, Harrison shuffled closer to Hayley, aware that she only wore a thin top and jacket.

"It's personal, isn't it? The reason you hate all of this so much." She asked, waving a hand toward the young couple wrapped up in each other nearby.

He studied her, watching for a hint of judgment, but he found none. Only curiosity and the familiar amber in her eyes.

It wasn't often he chose to open himself up to another. Usually it took Courier in size twelve to do it. Maybe it was how unabashedly she watched him or the easy space around them, like he'd stepped out of his normal life for a moment, right into celluloid. Some of the more resilient trees were sprouting early, fighting the cool temperature to show new life, and it reminded him so sharply of Em that his answer slipped forth easily.

"My sister," he says, clearing the emotion from his throat. "Emilia. She's ten months older, but everyone always thought we were twins because of how close we were."

Emilia would love this. Not the story itself, but him telling it. She had always accused him of being too distrusting. No doubt she and Hayley would get on like a house on fire.

"She was popular in school, had her share of boyfriends. But nothing ever worked out long term. When she graduated from college and still hadn't found the love her life, she wasn't worried. Said her plan was to start a family by thirty, and that still left plenty of time. And even on her thirtieth birthday, when her boyfriend said he never wanted kids, she broke it off and said that it was okay. Forty is the new thirty, apparently."

Life could be so fucking cruel. It was painful to watch her hope rise and fall with every failed date, every short-lived relationship. Yet she still believed in love. He couldn't understand it.

"What happened?" Hayley asked, her voice soft.

He stared down at his hands, noticed her knee resting against his. "She did what most hopeful singles do when they're trying to find love. She joined an app."

He turned his head, watching the soft tendrils of her hair as the wind brushed her face, her familiar scent washing over him. Her beautiful eyes were locked with his, filled with compassion. She was just so... good. He could change the subject right now, make a joke or stand without a word, and she wouldn't stop him. Wouldn't push.

He didn't quite have the words to thank her, but he wished he had.

"His name was Calvin Boyd. Said he worked on Wall Street, had a high-profile job that required a lot of travel and made it hard to settle down, but he'd always wanted the whole picture-perfect deal — wife, kids, dog, house."

"Sounds perfect," she said.

"Oh, that's nothing. He was the epitome of romance — sent her big bouquets of flowers, took her out to fancy dinners when he was in town, surprised her with gifts, sent her poetry every morning. They were already talking about moving in together after a couple of weeks."

"That's incredibly sudden. How did your sister feel about it?"

"She was head over heels for him. Convinced he was the one. Wouldn't hear a bad word about him. Even after he started asking her for money."

"Oh, no."

Bile still stung his throat when he thought about it. "Apparently, he was going through a nasty divorce that meant his assets were tied up. Which was a huge load of bullshit, but Emilia bought it. It was only after he'd drained her savings account and put her in thousands of dollars of credit card debt that she learned the truth."

"Where is he now?"

"Who knows. The cops said she isn't the only one he tricked, but it's almost impossible to get him on anything because everything was in her name." He hated that he couldn't do more for his sister. He hadn't been able to protect her.

And now he would be contributing to the same false promises that had left her vulnerable to a creep like that.

"So you can understand why I hate all this stuff." He gestured around them, although even he had to admit it was a beautiful spot.

"She's lucky to have you looking out for her." Hayley hugged herself, shivering.

He slipped off his coat and draped it over her shoulders. "Emilia is my best friend. She was there when…" He sighed. "I owe a lot to her."

Hayley considered him before placing her hand on his arm gently. An offer of support. "What was it for you?"

Of course she knew there was more. "Fifth grade. Couple of kids had been taunting me for most of the year, and one day, they decided to up the ante. They'd already broken my nose when Emilia stepped in. She's got a mean right hook."

Hayley smiled, but it was rife with past pain. Harrison knew that smile. Had seen it in the mirror many times.

"It was university for me," she said. "I grew up north of London, in a town south of Yorkshire. The people there, you may not realize, have very distinct accents. Thanks to a lot of hard work and the benefit of my family's position, I studied literature at Oxford."

The way she spoke was clear, polished. Practiced. Harrison's gut clenched.

"It was exciting. I'd graduated top of my class, and it was my dream to attend. It didn't take long to see that it didn't matter how smart I was. I was an outsider." She ducked her face, hiding behind her hair. "I spent every day practicing to talk like everybody else. Now I barely remember what I used to sound like."

Harrison's gut clenched. Those fucking posh bastards. He knew the type. Boorish, classist assholes. Apparently, it didn't matter what country you came from; they manifested everywhere like weeds.

Hayley avoided his gaze but hadn't moved away. Harrison pressed his knee to hers. The corner of her mouth curled up, but her smile didn't last.

"I learned to hate all that snobbish crap about what is highbrow and lowbrow. As if it matters. What? You're more deserving because you like intellectual films instead of silly little stories about love?"

Ouch. Harrison deserved that. He'd been a fucking asshole yesterday. And shit, he might not have the same love for the genre that she had, but hadn't he been the one to protest that all stories deserved to be heard?

She placed her hand on his, her voice soft with understanding. "For what it's worth, Harry, I understand why your sister still believes. Sometimes hope is as good as happiness, especially when we are striving for something we're not sure we'll ever have."

Her perfume was faint and sweet, the tease of a memory.

Harrison had always gravitated toward interesting people, but there was so much more to Hayley. The way her mind worked, her creativity, the slow, easy way she could connect ideas that would never occur to him. He was too methodical, too analytical. Hayley's mind oper-

46

ated like a current, smooth and calm. It fascinated him. Seduced him.

It had been easier before to tell himself that all he felt was physical, that the way she wore her heart on her sleeve, wove compassion into her words — scripted or otherwise — hadn't affected him.

But any attempt to pretend that was true was impossible when she was beside him, offering comfort for Emilia, looking like she wanted to hunt down the asshole who had hurt her and to give him his just desserts.

As the breeze passed, her hair fell across her face. On instinct, he reached out to tuck it behind her ear, relishing the softness of her skin and the way she leaned into his touch.

God, the curve of her neck did wicked things to him.

"Harry…"

A high squeal nearby cut Hayley off, and Harrison turned, afraid of what he'd find. A talking frog, hoping for the kiss that would turn him into a prince?

Instead, one half of the couple nearby was kneeling to propose to her girlfriend. A photographer closed in on them, beaming, and Harrison found himself smiling.

It was surprisingly sweet.

Music started, loud and insistent, and then, as if in slow motion, the crowd around them — every single person in the courtyard but the two of them — turned in a single synchronized movement.

"Oh look," Hayley said softly, while Harrison shuddered.

Because he could deal with a lot of things.

A week writing a romance film with a woman he had extremely inconvenient feelings for.

Crazy coffee shop moments and a city obsessed with Valentine's Day.

But he would not, *could not*, handle a flash mob.

"Oh hush, it's sweet," Hayley chided, poking him where he was most ticklish. "It's not like they're asking you to join in."

And thank god for that.

The couple watched on with gleeful expressions. Clearly they didn't have a problem with it. He couldn't imagine wanting a spectacle like this if someone proposed to him.

Hayley leaned in. Heat radiated along his side where they touched. "Of course you can't. Some of us find it utterly romantic. Putting aside your ego so you can announce how you feel about someone? That's bravery."

"Some of us prefer our dignity," he lied. Emilia would probably kick his ass if she heard him.

When Hayley frowned and pulled away, he fought the urge to shuffle closer.

21 EXT. COURTYARD — DAY

    Dancers are now all around them. A cover of "I Get A Kick Out Of You" blasts from a speaker.

———

The whole dance scenario was as ridiculous as yesterday's coffee shop disaster. If he didn't know any better, he'd think he was dreaming. Writing often caused his mind to create odd scenarios, his subconscious filling in the blanks.

But never in his most fevered creative state would he create a flash mob, especially one with such bad direction (at least a third of the dancers were out of time). If the characters in his head were going to choreograph a dance, they would at least hit their marks.

Considering his recent luck, he shouldn't have been surprised when a nearby dancer pulled him off the bench to join in.

And maybe, if he hadn't been shocked, he wouldn't have tripped over his own feet in an effort to pull away.

Maybe, if he wasn't having the strangest week of his life, he wouldn't have fallen ass over head into a damn fountain, but he was pretty sure Hayley was right, and he was paying karmic restitution. Who was he to question the laws of the universe?

This was how Hayley found him — soggy and contrite. "Go ahead. I know I look ridiculous."

"I'm sorry," she laughed, ducking to the side when he splashed her.

"No, you're not. You're full of tea and no sympathy." Finally, he succumbed to the ridiculousness, laughing at himself.

He deserved the comeuppance for every dig she'd tolerated over the last forty-eight hours. But he could have handled learning his lesson without ruining half his wardrobe in the process. And what was it about these damn clichés that so often ended up with someone needing to get undressed after?

Oh.

Actually, that made sense. Maybe there really was something to all this nonsense.

"Do you need a hand?"

She'd said something similar the night they'd slept together.

He looked up at Hayley, her hand held out, the shared memory dancing in her eyes. She was framed beautifully, the perfect blue of the sky and the light of the sun. If he wouldn't look unhinged, he would stay put and search for the right words to capture the moment.

He longed to transform these moments to film, their brightness always dulled in the adaptation. Far easier for him to capture pain, regret, disappointment.

Hope, happiness, love... Harrison barely knew where to start.

———

Curious stares followed them on their walk back. The judgment of his half-soaked state prickled against his skin. He should be furious. These were his favorite jeans.

But with every look he chanced at Hayley, he caught her smiling back, and the wall he'd been about to erect disappeared.

"That was embarrassing," he admitted.

"More embarrassing than the time you attempted to sing a Prince song at that karaoke bar?"

Color dotted the high points of her cheekbones. It took all of his self-control not to explore the warmth of them with his lips.

"Says the woman who couldn't remember the lyrics to "Wannabe." I'm surprised they didn't take your citizenship after that."

"Oh, they tried," Hayley joked. "I had to name all the members of *Monty Python* and recite every word to an Adele song for them to let me back in again."

Harrison's bark of laughter caused a man walking past them to jump, but he couldn't bring himself to apologize.

"This is the second shirt I've had ruined in two days," he said, shivering. "I'm going to run out of clothes."

"I fail to see an issue with that," Hayley said, a gleam in her eye.

How he wanted to follow down the path where that gleam lead.

Then she continued, "With your wardrobe, it's a kindness to destroy them."

Wednesday

Normal was a terrible word. What was normal to one person was strange to someone else, and people were historically shitheads to anyone who wasn't normal.

So, yeah. Fuck normal.

In his experience, strange was almost always infinitely better.

But this week?

Harrison would have given his left nut for normal.

He didn't even believe in karma. Waiting for come-uppance was a one-way street to disappointment. But what else could explain why he was suddenly facing the consequences of his actions? From the moment Hayley had walked into that room, he'd done nothing but fight her. Getting dunked in a fountain was the least he deserved.

It was a testament to Hayley's kindness that she put up with him.

Her gaze snapped up to him as he stepped into the meeting room, her eyes widening as she stilled. "What are you wearing?"

He threw himself into a chair, ignoring the way her shoulders shook with repressed laughter.

Harrison scowled harder.

"You know, normally when a woman asks me that, she's a little less amused."

When he had sent Monday's shirt to be laundered, he expected — irrationally, it turned out — that it would be returned without issue. Instead, he had been sent an apology note and a very bright — and tight — pink sweatshirt, with the phrase "it's how you use it that counts" encased in a heart.

A few days ago, he'd never even *heard* of a Valentine's festival, and now it was the bane of Harrison's existence.

"Contrary to popular belief, no amount of brooding will help us finish this manuscript faster. So you can take your dark and sexy artist act elsewhere."

"You think I look sexy?" Harrison winked, feeling victorious when Hayley's cheeks darkened.

"You look ridiculous."

"I don't know; you said sexy first." He leaned back, propping his feet on the table. "Maybe we should talk about this."

"Maybe," she said, closing the distance to push his feet back to the floor, "we could focus on the job at hand so that we might finish the script."

"How hard can it be? We're almost done." He gestured at the mosaic of notes littering the wall. "In fact, I bet I could finish this on my own."

Hayley stood between his legs. "Come on, Harry. I thought you knew better than to bet against me by now."

"Rewriting history again? I won that last round —"

"On a technicality."

He shrugged, pleased. "Don't care. Still counts."

"I seem to remember you conceding that point once."

"Yeah, well, I wasn't thinking straight at the time."

Mostly because he'd been buried deep in her and five seconds away from coming harder than he had in years.

"If I remember correctly, you haven't thought straight since you were about nine years old."

That was true.

He couldn't keep the grin off his face. "Doesn't change the fact that I won. What are you afraid of?"

"Where you're concerned? Not much." Hayley's smile widened until her eyes were almost hidden by her cheeks. "Can we get back to work, please?"

"If you think you can work without getting distracted by all my sexy brooding."

He ducked out of the way of the sugar packet.

———

"We can't set the whole thing at one convention. That's maybe three days, tops. That's not enough time. Not if you want the audience to think it's going to last."

Hayley slapped his hand, batting it away from the Post-it he'd hoped to remove. "So we give them a little personal history."

Finally. As it stood, they were pretty thin cutouts of people, and a decent backstory would go a long way. A life lived, just out of frame.

Hayley held out her pen to him. He tried to ignore how often he'd seen it touch her lips.

Her hair was tied up today, the soft hem of her white shirt accentuating the slope of her neck. Her pale skin held a subtle glow. It had to be a trick. Nothing glowed under hotel lighting. And yet he couldn't look away.

She waited. "You're the character expert."

Gauntlet thrown, he took the pen from her. It didn't matter that this wasn't the sort of film he'd ever watch, because she knew his weakness — the creative itch. The inescapable call to get into the sandbox and make something out of nothing.

"The quickest way is to make them more familiar. This isn't the first time they've been pitted against each other, but it is the first time they've had to work together. Then," he said, pulling a note off the wall,

"instead of the turning point of act two being accidental, we change it so that she sets him up to fail."

He turned, struck by the force of Hayley's attention. Even after listening to him complain for two days straight, here she was, waiting with open curiosity, asking for his opinion.

Harrison cleared his throat, turning back to the wall. "She wants to prove that he's the wrong person to sell it, right? So she tells him on purpose that it does something it can't or hears him mention it and doesn't correct him. But when they lose the account, she realizes she fucked up. So when they argue about each other's methods, she's feeling guilty, even though she still thinks he should think before he acts."

Hayley was nodding more enthusiastically now, her pen moving feverishly across a series of notes. "Actually, that's perfect. And maybe when she begs the buyer to give them another chance, she employs some of his methods —"

"Letting her see the value in what he does," Harrison finished.

Five new notes went up, filling in the end of act two and the beginning of act three. Hayley beamed, and the power of the expression stalled his heart for a brief moment.

"That was genius. You really are good at this."

The compliment zipped up his spine. He should be hating this. He wanted to hate this. But it was becoming hard to remember the reasons he should.

He'd never enjoyed writing with someone else. Too many egos at play. When no one wanted to compromise, the resulting film was chaotic. It almost never felt collaborative, and it annoyed him to know he might never have this again.

It was good — too good — the way they worked together. And in a few short days, he'd have to go back to his old ways, pretending he wasn't missing out.

That he wasn't missing her.

"I didn't add much. You came up with most of it." His voice had dropped to a whisper.

She brushed his hand with hers, the glide of her fingers along his skin gentle. "I mean it, Harry. Thank you. I'm really glad you agreed to stay."

The distance between them had shrunk. He itched to slide a hand around her waist, tangle the other in her hair. No doubt she'd taste like tea and sugar.

"Me, too."

———

After ten minutes of tapping, Harrison was ready to take it back.

Hayley had been staring at the third act, her tea cold, and her pen keeping time. She had something on her mind, and as much as Harrison wanted to leave her to her creative process, it was getting to him.

Then it stopped.

"I think we need to change the climax. You were right; it's too idyllic."

Harrison looked up in surprise. Monday, she'd fought against changing it. "What about what the audience wants? I thought you said —"

"I know, and there'll need to be a sense of grandeur. But I keep thinking about what you said yesterday, and you're right. Love isn't solely about the big moments. What is it that really makes us fall for someone? It's the little things, the way they listen and take care of you, when they support you without needing to change who you are. I want to show that."

He wasn't sure what to say. She had no reason to placate him, yet here she was, going out of her way to change the script.

Because of him.

"Okay." He swallowed. "But if we're going to do this, I don't want to sell a lie."

"We won't. I promise you that, Harry. I want to write a love story that isn't a dream. I want it to be hopeful. Sweet. Maybe a little sexy." She reached over, her palm warm on his wrist. She stroked a comforting line into his skin with her thumb. "I want something real."

Her eyes were imploring. He wanted to get lost in them.

"It's okay for you to want it too, Harry."

Fuck.

She was hope, heaven, like a fucking goldmine at the end of a rainbow, and Harrison did want, more than anything. But the sharp, jagged edges of his humor weren't all for show. He really was curt and pessimistic and ready to rage at every piece of the world that was broken and overlooked while people posted clickbait headlines and fretted over egos. His heart wanted, but it was covered in thorns. And Hayley was bound to get cut in the process. He wouldn't do that. Wouldn't be the asshole who disappointed her.

He couldn't offer her anything close to what she deserved, so why torture himself? It had been hard enough trying to forget her the first time. He needed to stop messing around and focus on the work.

So he turned away, digging his fingernails into his palms and hating again that life was nothing like the movies.

26 INT. HOTEL — MEETING ROOM — DAY

Harrison and Hayley are sitting directly across from each other, eyes locked, neither willing to concede.

———

"No. I've already agreed to the last-minute chase down, but a public declaration? It's not realistic." On that point, he was determined. He wanted his dignity intact after this was released.

Hayley slow blinked, her nostrils flaring. "It's supposed to be aspirational."

"Fine, but don't expect me to help."

"Oh, I'm not expecting *anything* from you, Harry."

Being this close to her was lighting up all his danger signs.

Worse than that, there was no space to move in this damn room, no way to keep his distance. He had kicked the table at least four separate times trying to move out of her way. His shin was in agony.

Hayley had gotten quieter as the day progressed, shooting him glances when she thought he wasn't looking, her shoulders set high and tight. The marks on her pen where she chewed becoming more numerous as time passed, even after he'd risked a visit back to the coffee shop of doom and returned with tea and cake.

Despite that, the script was actually coming together. The wall was now littered with notes, a bright mosaic he'd started wistfully staring at in order to avoid looking across the table.

And still, Hayley's frown deepened.

Focusing on the script should have helped. He'd stopped complaining long enough to be helpful, or so he'd thought.

Maybe she'd finally had enough of him. Seen this as the disaster he'd proclaimed it to be. It shouldn't have hurt as much as it did.

He was clearly out of his depth — not a surprise. Opening his mouth around Hayley had only ever gotten him into trouble.

So why had she been punching the keys on her laptop like they offended her? The crease of her brow was so pronounced it made him nervous.

Blessedly, a knock sounded at the door, cutting into their fourth debate of the day.

Harrison balled his hand into a fist, staring Hayley down. "I don't care if it's expected. I'll let a miscommunication trope into this script over my cold, dead body."

She was practically vibrating with frustration. "Oh, you're so…"

He was sure Hayley was going to throw her tea at him.

He was even more sure that he deserved it.

"Sexy? Suave? Right?"

"More like frustrating, arrogant, and pessimistic."

The door opened. It was the hotel manager. Harrison sat straighter. "Not again."

"So sorry to bother you, but we've had another problem with the rooms."

"Of course you have. What now? A visiting prince in disguise? A rockstar with a bleak past and a heart of gold? A wisecracking waitress who can't access her inheritance unless she gets married?"

"That last one's pretty good actually," Hayley said, taking notes.

"Actually, it's a problem with Ms. Bennett's room."

Her head whipped up so fast it was comical. Harrison had to bite back a laugh. It sure felt good to not be on the receiving end of her glare for once.

"I'm so sorry, but we had a system failure this morning, and it recorded you as checked out."

"So check me back in."

"I'm afraid I can't. One of our trainees checked another couple into the room an hour ago. I'm trying to sort it out, but I don't have any other rooms right now. I know you and Mr. Kyle are close, so I sent your bags up to his suite."

Now she was staring at Harrison. "Suite?"

Shit. He hadn't planned on mentioning that.

The manager placed a card on the table. "I went ahead and made an extra key. I'll just leave you two. Sorry again."

Sure he was.

```
DISSOLVE TO:

   27   INT.    BALLROOM    —    EVENING
(FLASHBACK)


OMITTED
```

Hayley ripped the Post-it off the wall, pinning Harrison with an unimpressed stare while she pressed the square into his chest. "You can't cut to a flashback halfway through the narrative, Harry."

Frankly, it was a little harsh. "Why not? No one will be expecting that."

"Yes. For good reason." She turned back to the wall, tapping her pen against a lone pink note they needed to place. "Now, can we please decide when they're going to have sex? If they dance around each other any more, we're going to give the audience blue balls."

They wouldn't be the only ones suffering.

Probably not a good time to remind her that they would be sharing a room later.

The same generic pop song was playing in the elevator again. Beside him, Hayley was silent, but it was far from comfortable.

She stood stiff, silent, avoiding contact with him and staring straight ahead. He missed the teasing from yesterday and kicked himself for making a hard week harder. Somehow he'd managed to annoy her more by trying to work together than he had when he'd been messing around.

He should say something. He was tempted to make a joke, but the muscles in her jaw were locked tight, and her arms barricaded her chest. He wasn't willing to risk bodily harm if he got it wrong and made it worse.

As promised, Hayley's suitcase was awaiting them. Along with a few other things.

"Do you have something to tell me, Harry?" Hayley said, staring at the bed.

Harrison didn't know what to focus on first. The twin towels that were curved into kissing swans? The box of chocolates? The rose petals?

That fucking manager had it out for him.

"No champagne, I see," she added, sounding somewhere between amused and disappointed.

He risked a glance at her. There was a hint of a smile playing on her lips, and the sight of it flooded him with relief.

"That was yesterday. Wait until tomorrow; I've heard the violinist is quite talented."

As he'd hoped, her resolve cracked, joy spreading across her features and lighting Harrison up from the inside out.

She studied the bed again, and Harrison flushed. In a few hours, they'd be sleeping here.

In this bed.

Together.

He cleared his throat, turning away. "I'll let you unpack. How do you feel about room service?"

———

Hayley was beside herself as he recounted the strange list of events he'd suffered through, at one point laughing so hard she snorted.

Suddenly, every embarrassing story he had begged to be told. Anything to keep her smiling at him.

"I'm starting to think Cupid has a vendetta against you," Hayley said, dipping a fry into her curry.

"I can't imagine what I've done to piss him off," he joked, taking a bite of his burger and trying not to spill half its contents on himself. He refused to ruin another shirt.

Refused.

Hayley beamed over the room service tray. She looked especially sexy, wearing a set of navy silk pajamas that clung to her breasts and ass in a way designed purely with Harrison's fraying nerves in mind.

"How do you know Cupid is a him?"

Harrison considered. "Regularly causes mischief, shoots first and thinks later…" That got a laugh from her, and he busied his hands before he could pull her onto his lap.

"Now it's starting to sound like you have a personal grudge."

Harrison huffed a laugh. "Maybe I do."

There must have been something in his voice, some hint behind the joke, but then maybe not — Hayley had always seen through his bullshit — because she was studying him, carefully, curious.

"You've never been in love, have you?"

"I thought I was once." Even though he expected her surprise, it still made him smile. "I know, me of all people."

"Of all people," she repeated, teasing. "What happened?"

"Timing," was all he was willing to say. "How about you?"

"Yes, I've been in love." When she didn't add any more, he wanted to ask. Wanted to know everything. Who was this guy? What happened?

"You're not with him now." This was the most important part.

Her expression shifted, too complicated for him to interpret. "No. We're not involved at the moment."

"See? Cupid has a lot to answer for."

She gave him a small, warm smile. "Love is one of the most amazing experiences you'll ever have. There's nothing like it. You can't plan it or plot it or teach yourself. It just happens. Like breathing."

"I disagree. Love is learned. How else do you think Valentine's Day became a thing? Or those love locks on bridges? None of that existed before someone invented them."

"You're missing the point, as usual. All that fluff is a byproduct, ways the world has found to express it. But love itself is… uncontainable. When you feel it, it pours out of you. In every word, in every gesture. You'll find more and more ways of articulating it because you'll go mad otherwise. You'll say it over and over because you can't help yourself." She paused to shake her head. "It won't even change when they frustrate the hell out of you. Every little thing makes you love even more."

"But it's finite. No energy is everlasting, not even love. So what's the point?"

Her eyes bored into him. He wished he saw it the same. He was broken, knew it with every fiber of his being, and he'd been okay with that. But right now, faced with the naked hope in her eyes, passion coming off her in waves, he wished he wasn't.

"The point, Harry, is to feel it."

Maybe that's why he was so bitter about it. Because despite all his complaining, every sneer, every eye roll, every groan… he was jealous. And he hated it.

Harrison wasn't the guy people wanted forever with.

All this shit?

The false hope, the cutesy posts, the happily-ever-afters?

It was all designed to leave you kicked in the gut when it never happened to you.

"I have to ask you something."

She pushed her plate away, laying her napkin over it. "Am I going to get mad?"

Harrison chuckled. "It's highly likely."

To his joy, she smiled and shrugged. "Go ahead then."

"You honestly believe in meeting the one, don't you? True love, soulmates, all that crap."

"Yes," she said, without embarrassment.

"Why?"

The real question was, could she ever imagine being with someone who didn't — couldn't — believe?

"Because I choose to. Because it has less to do with luck and stumbling onto the perfect person and so much more to do with the act of love. Every day we have the opportunity to practice loving in all sorts of ways that have nothing to do with looks or money or sex and everything to do with compassion and kindness and respect."

Had Harrison ever heard anyone talk like that before? With such conviction? Everything in his chest felt too tight, his own heart practically giving Hayley a standing ovation, thumping loudly against his ribcage, in his throat.

No wonder her films were so popular. If she could make an audience feel an iota of what she made him feel...

She brushed a crumb off the table. "I think that there are people out there whom we are uniquely suited for, but those people are rare. So if the opportunity arises, you can't let it slip through your fingers. When I've met someone I care for," his breath caught as her gaze met his, "I don't run away."

He swallowed back the lump in his throat.

This was why he'd never wanted this project. She'd always managed to find her way behind enemy lines, no matter how fortified his defenses were. Hard to keep her out when he was the one handing her the damn key.

"You know that all this stuff," he waved at the gifts the hotel had left them, "is made up. A series of carefully crafted moments specifically designed to manipulate the audience. And you're okay with that?"

"Yes," she said. "I want the whole mad dance, from rain kisses to public declarations. Someone to care for me when I'm sick, save me from attending another boring event, or simply be quiet with. I want it all."

And dammit, the more time he spent with her, the harder it was to not want it, too.

30 INT. HOTEL - BEDROOM - NIGHT

———

Preparing for sleep was an exercise in restraint. Hayley slipped into the bathroom to brush her teeth before Harrison showered. He was hard as fuck, but he would not jack off while she was in the next room. Even if it meant taking the coldest shower he could stand.

He hoped she'd be asleep when he returned and they wouldn't have to face the awkward moment when they would lie next to each other, not discussing the obvious.

Maybe he should sleep on the couch.

He exited the bathroom in his boxers and T-shirt. No fucking way he was sleeping naked tonight. A single lamp illuminated the room, casting a soft, seductive glow over the bed. Despite his attempts to discourage his dick from getting any ideas, it stubbornly refused to go completely soft, and it wouldn't take a genius to tell that from looking at him.

So, of course, it was the first thing Hayley noticed when he walked into the bedroom.

She was sitting against the headboard on the left side of the bed, notepad in her lap, when her gaze jumped up to greet him, noticeably snagging on his package. His dick, the traitor, thickened at the attention.

Six months ago, while they had fucked in that coat room, he'd thought about this. About having her in a bed, laid out so he could take his time. Testing how far he could tease her before she couldn't take it anymore.

Seeing whether their fantasies aligned.

"Maybe I should sleep on the couch."

"Don't be ridiculous, Harry. You wouldn't even fit comfortably. If anyone should sleep on the couch —"

"You're not sleeping on the couch." He was not that much of an asshole.

"Then I guess you'd better get in."

In three long strides, Harrison was standing at the right side of the bed. He pulled back the covers, slipped in, and turned onto his side, his eyes and his dick facing away from her.

It was going to be a very long night.

"Goodnight, Harry."

Did she always have to say his name like that? It wasn't helping.

"Goodnight."

Her chuckle followed, before quiet scratches of her pen against paper were the only sounds in the room. After a while, a light humming started up. She probably wasn't even aware she was doing it.

And all of a sudden — the routine, the silent maneuvering, the easy comfort — he could imagine it. Night after night, together, just like this.

And dammit, he wanted it.

The humming stopped, replaced by the sounds of Hayley setting her notebook and pen on the nightstand. Then the last remaining light went out.

He could feel the heat of her at his back, even with the carefully placed distance between them. He wanted to turn, reach out, trace the curve of her cheek, her lips, with his hands, then his tongue.

It would be so easy to follow through, pull her close. Taste the subtle sweetness of her neck, the very thing that had been distracting him for days.

In the end, it was the sound of her steady breathing that sent him to sleep. The lingering scent of jasmine, the mint from her toothpaste.

The memory of her in his arms.

Thursday

W hen Harrison woke, it was to a warm body in his arms and his nose buried in a familiar scent. Soft, silky. Sweet. He pulled it closer, eyes still closed, taking a deep breath.

The body he held hummed sleepily, shifting until it was rubbing deliciously against his dick. He pressed into it, the friction making him harder, until he heard a familiar sigh. Instantly aware, he froze — now fully awake — remembering who he'd slept next to.

Who he'd been cuddling.

Shit.

He should have known he couldn't trust his dick. Give it an inch and it would take seven more.

God, he wanted her. How perfectly they fit together. The breathy sounds she made when he was inside her. The way she smelled, warm and fragrant and real.

But after last time, he'd promised himself he'd back off. Being with Hayley was so much more than sex. It was the way her smile spread across her face, how she lit up while she worked, the triumph in her eyes when she came up with a line that was particularly perfect.

The secret little pat on the back she sometimes gave herself when she solved a problem and thought no one was looking.

How easy-going she could be, casually changing course when he suggested altering something, as long as it benefited the script.

Whereas the last thing he felt right now was casual. About any of it.

Slowly, he eased off, a difficult task since Hayley sleepily followed him. It was more than he could stand, his dick so freaking hard he was worried if he fell the wrong way out of bed, he would break the damn thing. Which it honestly deserved since it had gotten him into this mess in the first place.

Eventually, he was free, already on his way to the bathroom as Hayley's alarm went off. He locked the door and glared at himself in the mirror.

The first chance he got, he was going to find that damn manager and get her room back.

Because he wasn't sure he — or his dick — could handle another night in that bed with her.

————

He spent breakfast waiting for Hayley to bring up that morning, but she never did, forcing Harrison to accept that he was the only one affected.

Although there had been a few moments where he'd hoped otherwise.

Loitering at the breakfast buffet, he messaged Emilia.

H: Think I've made a huge mistake.

She called immediately.

"Please tell me you're being your usual level of

dramatic and don't need a lawyer. I need to know how nice I have to be to you."

"I can't do it."

It had been on his mind since yesterday, especially as Hayley's mood turned. He'd been dragging them down since the beginning. Maybe leaving would be best for both of them.

Surely the studio would understand. And he could use the extra time to ask himself some hard questions.

"Do you think I write movies that make people cry in the shower?"

"Wow," Emilia said, the sound drawn out. "I... What did Hayley say to you?"

"It's not her." He ignored the snort of disbelief on the other end. "I've just been thinking a lot since I got here, about what I'm doing. Who am I writing for? What am I trying to achieve?"

"Those are pretty big questions for a Thursday morning. Have you found the answers yet?"

Across the restaurant, Hayley was smiling brightly, talking with a server while they refilled Harrison's cup.

"Maybe. But I think I've been avoiding them."

By the time he returned to the table, her attention was buried in her notebook. The familiar sight made Harrison smile. He couldn't remember the last time he'd wanted to savor the morning like this.

The coffee refreshed him, and he relaxed. Until something pressed lightly against his calf.

He looked across to Hayley, who was still writing, focusing on her notebook like nothing was amiss, her expression soft, serene. Except that was definitely her foot curled around his leg. Not moving, just… anchored. Connected.

Harrison shifted enough to press back — *good morning* — heat jolting through him when her lips curled a little extra in response.

He downed the rest of his coffee.

"Want to get out of here for a bit?"

Her smile was blinding. "Desperately."

———

Tuesday, they'd turned left, so today they went right, leaving the hotel for the riverside. While evidence of the Valentine's festivities continued to dominate every inch of the city, it grew impossibly more incessant the farther they walked, all signs pointing — in some cases, literally — to the fairgrounds, where marquees and stalls were being erected for Saturday.

As they approached the entrance, Harrison spotted what had drawn Hayley there. A 50s-era Cadillac in bright pink was parked on the grass, the front doors and trunk open and overflowing with flowers.

"Mmm, it must be nice."

Harrison glanced over, but Hayley's attention was squarely on the display. Keeping watch, he hummed, curious.

"The one time I received flowers, I sent them to myself." Hayley bit her lower lip, and Harrison fought to keep his attention on what she was saying. "All through high school, I had a crush on my best friend, but he wanted someone else. I sent myself a bouquet with a fake card, hoping he'd get jealous, but…" Her arm brushed his when she shrugged. "It was exactly as pathetic as it sounds."

It killed him that her smile didn't reach her eyes. He wanted to find this asshole and make him pay. Then drive that entire ridiculous flower car over to the hotel and stuff their room full of the blooms.

"It's not pathetic at all."

And before he could overthink it, he laced their hands together and walked them straight over to the car.

Beside it stood a woman with a skull-patterned blouse and a conflicted look on her face.

"Morning," she said as they approached. "You wouldn't happen to be Wanda's friends, would you?"

"Oh. I'm sorry, no," Hayley answered, sounding genuinely disappointed that they weren't.

Harrison reined in a smile.

The woman, Charlie, explained that she was a few helpers short. "At this rate, we won't make the festival at all."

Hayley was admiring a large display, packed to the brim with flowers. "These are beautiful. Will they last the weekend?"

"Oh yeah, they're all fake. It's the only way to keep them photo ready for the next three days. You'd be amazed by how many people will come to take a photo with the car."

It was official. Harrison was getting old. Not "kids these days" old, but he didn't understand the appeal. Sure, the car was beautiful, and the flowers too, but really?

"Oh yeah," Charlie said. "Actually, I need some promo shots for our socials. Care to be my guinea pigs?"

Hayley pinned him with a pleading look. "Harry?"

"Sure, why not?" He couldn't resist her. "Where do you need us?"

34 INT. CAR – DAY

———

The car was a hell of a lot smaller on the inside. Charlie had convinced Hayley that the best photos would be of the two of them cuddled up on the back seat.

So here they were.

"You're telling me people will voluntarily line up for hours just to take a single photo with some flowers?" Harrison grumbled, recognizing the scent of the hotel's shampoo in Hayley's hair. The overwhelming urge to get his hands in it gripped tight while she smirked up at him.

"Yep."

"And that's supposed to be enjoyable?"

Charlie laughed. "Yes."

Hayley clicked her tongue. "Don't listen to him. He's far less of a grinch than he's pretending to be."

The even battle of wills he'd been locked in for days was now a two against one situation. When Emilia met Hayley, he'd never win an argument again.

"Okay, that's it." Charlie looked at the phone's screen, then studied them again. "Harry, can you put your arm around Hayley's waist?"

He did as instructed, biting back a curse. Squeezed into the back seat of the Cadillac with a lap full of his co-writer, Harrison was revising his previous opinion on karma. Because surely this counted as some kind of physical torture.

Emotional, too.

"Great, now Hayley, can you turn your face — no, toward Harrison — lovely. Yes!"

Harrison kept his focus forward, all too aware of Hayley's... everything — her scent, the heat of her body, her breath hitting his neck — and the phone Charlie was no doubt using to capture his current turmoil. In 4K.

Fantastic.

"Okay, now Hayley, sit next to him, and I'm going to take a shot through the windshield, so I'll need you to snuggle up."

He was once again drawn to the curve of her neck, his gaze following the breadcrumbs of each freckle as they danced along her pale skin. More than anything, he wanted to settle his mouth against her pulse, simply rest his head and breathe her in.

And Christ, she was so warm. Her body fitting into his perfectly. It was familiar and new and so fucking intoxicating that he could barely think.

Every touch between them was impossible to ignore, his hand on her back, her palm on his thigh, the brush of her hair on his shoulder.

It made him want things he shouldn't. Breakfasts, lunches, dinners, late nights, lazy weekends, holidays, and everything in between. He wanted to traverse those freckles across every mile of her skin, navigate each sharp corner of her wit, sink into the warm sweetness of her love.

She was everything he'd ever hoped for and never believed he'd have.

Hayley shifted, her ass grazing his lap in a teasing reminder of that morning. Harrison stifled a groan. She shifted again.

He took a deep breath, hoping for a patience he didn't think existed. Just one more; then he could get out of this cramped space.

Harrison couldn't move, couldn't do anything except look at Hayley. His breathing was going haywire. The way her dark hair curled at her shoulders, her lips petal pink and inviting, he'd barely need to move to close the gap between them.

"What is it?" she whispered.

He wanted to reach for her. Pull her closer. Trap her mouth under his.

His bicep warmed where she pressed against it, a reminder that she'd been in his arms this morning.

Saying yes to her had never been a hardship. It was saying no that was the issue.

Charlie's yell was muffled. "This is great, guys. Keep going!"

"Two down," he said. "Two thousand to go."

"And you call me melodramatic."

He fought the urge to kiss her. It was becoming harder and harder to deny.

If only the lust that rolled through him every time she was near was the problem. If fucking her again was the goal, this week would be easy. A goddamn pleasure cruise. But he wouldn't be satisfied, couldn't deny how much he enjoyed simply being around her.

And he wanted more.

———

Two thousand hadn't been far off. By the time they'd made it out of the car and under the arch, Charlie must have had more than enough. But with every complaint, she simply kept insisting she needed "one more."

"Get really close. Stare into each other's eyes as though there'll never be another soul on earth worthy of your love."

Seriously. He wasn't some godforsaken cliché, ready to be manhandled into —

"Harry," Hayley whispered, cotton soft and oh so close. And he followed easily, like she must have known he would, their hips slotted together and his heart chasing a dream.

"Fantastic," Charlie said from somewhere. "How do you feel about a kiss?"

Good, was the truth.

And maybe he'd said it out loud, because Hayley was leaning in, leaving him the last few inches to cross on his own.

Some dreams weren't dreams at all, but destinations.

Her breath stuttered as he brushed a chaste kiss against her lips, wanting — always wanting — more. But how much of this was Hayley and how much the fantasy?

"So good, you guys."

Charlie's comment brought reality crashing back, and he pulled away.

Hayley was beautiful every day, but framed by a veritable meadow, she stunned. Her sweater was a deep blush that perfectly complemented her pale skin. A white shirt poked out from under the neckline, and both were tucked into her dark jeans.

He loosened his grip from her waist and ran his hands along her arms to her neck, noting how her pulse fluttered under his palm.

Hayley pulled a small bud from behind him and slipped it behind his ear, her eyes shining so brightly that Harrison worried the need to have her might break him apart.

"Hey, lovebirds," Charlie teased. "I'm not paying you to make eyes at each other."

"You're not paying us at all," Hayley laughed, tripping Harrison's heart further. The need to kiss her again was overwhelming. Brazenly, he traced his thumb along the line of her jaw. Hayley's expression softened, and she surprised him, turning to place a soft kiss on his palm, her eyes never leaving his.

"You heard the boss," she said, and he let his hands fall back to his sides, the hot press of her mouth a brand on his skin.

———

Eventually — how many photos of the same people could Charlie possibly need? — they were done.

He wanted to complain, but Charlie looked so relieved that he knew he couldn't.

"I can't thank you enough."

"It was our pleasure," Hayley said. "Do you want a hand loading your van up?"

"Absolutely," Charlie said but stayed behind when Hayley walked over to the car. She turned to him. "So…"

There was a glint in her eye. He wasn't sure he liked where this was going.

"How long have you two been together?"

He stared down at his hands. "We're not. We just work together."

"Uh-huh. Sure. You forget that I spend almost all my time around couples. Do you know how many weddings I've done where the groom looks at his wife the way you look at her?"

As if needing to prove her wrong, Harrison turned his attention to Hayley, trying to school his features into something resembling apathy. He managed it, mostly, and then a passing wind blew a bloom into the path of a man with a young child on his shoulders. Harrison watched him pass the flower back to Hayley, a short conversation occurring.

He'd had plenty of opportunities to watch Hayley from afar. He relied on his habit of people watching for his work, but it was different with her. Hayley drew him in no matter how crowded the room. Once he found her, he couldn't look away.

She was soft where he was all edges. Patient where he was irritable.

She made him want to be better.

"I knew it," Charlie said. She pressed her lips together and tapped her fingertips in quiet applause, bouncing in place. "I could tell the minute you two showed up. You're so cute together. She's sunshine; you're rain. The perfect combination."

"Okay, you've lost me. But congratulations on your imagination."

Charlie laughed. "You're in love with her."

He narrowed his eyes. "Nice try."

"If your answer was no, you wouldn't be so afraid to admit it. Just saying."

"What are you, some kind of love guru?"

"Like I said, I'm a fan of romance."

"Isn't everybody."

"You should tell her."

"Tell me what?" Hayley appeared, surprising him. Flushed and happy, she looked so beautiful he ached.

"You've got pollen in your hair."

"And you are a terrible liar," she said. "Fine, don't tell me. I have other ways of getting it out of you."

He had no doubt about that. Hayley could get him to do anything she damn well wanted.

———

Lee had been telling him for years that he had a habit of getting a little too deep into his work. Maybe he was right. Maybe all this talk about love and romance and relationships had rewired his brain. Although that didn't explain the suite. Or the coffee shop. Or the impromptu dance number.

Or that he had been feeling this way since long before this week.

The moment he crossed the threshold, Harrison went straight for the minibar.

The towel swans had returned tonight, neatly arranged on their bed.

He practically gulped from his wineglass, trying to avoid thoughts about the looks and touches they'd shared today, the lack of space between them, how close he was to giving in to how much he wanted her.

Harrison finished his glass of wine. Poured another.

He hadn't faced his opinions on love in a long time. And he knew what he would find if he did. But if he couldn't be honest with himself, he was no better than a hypocrite. His work hinged on digging below the surface. On asking why. On challenging it.

"You know," Hayley said, voice low in the quiet. "I've been waiting for you to yell at me."

Dinner had been eaten and cleared quickly, with conversation hovering over all kinds of unimportant topics. Without discussing it, they'd ended up beside each other on the couch, though neither one of them had made a move to turn the TV on.

They should talk about today, about this whole damn week, but Harrison hadn't found the right words yet.

A writer with no words. He should be ashamed.

"Why would I do that?"

"Because I'm the reason you're here. I asked for you. They wanted to pass the job off to someone who had more experience writing solo and only agreed to let me stay on if I worked with a co-writer."

What bullshit.

"You asked for me?"

The crease returned, jagged between her brows. "Is that really so surprising? I wanted to see you again."

He was lost for words. His heart kicked out of beat, his breathing rushing to catch up. Months of avoiding her, attempting to forget her before he got hurt, only to end up here.

She'd asked for him.

He really was an idiot.

"I didn't think you'd want to see me after…"

Hurt flashed across her face. "Was it really that bad?"

He moved closer — was helpless not to — brushing his fingers along her forearm. "If you really believe that, I definitely need to up my game."

Finally, finally, her brow cleared, one cheek lifting as she smiled. "I can assure you, you don't."

When his fingers passed her wrist, she curled her hand around his, and as her gaze fell to his lips, he stilled, waiting for her to follow through.

But she didn't.

"More wine?" she asked, standing to retrieve the bottle.

And look. Maybe he did judge too quickly. Maybe he buried himself in work too often and overthought probably everything, but he knew interest when it smacked him in the face.

He hadn't *forgotten* that she had wanted him, too. He'd just… been ignoring the fact. Because Harrison didn't do anything by halves. Once he knew he wanted something, he jumped in. Deep end, fully clothed, whatever.

And he wanted to jump for Hayley.

But he'd never given himself permission to hope that she would want it back.

And now that she might? Well, it would take a better man than Harrison to say no.

38 INT. HOTEL - BATHROOM - NIGHT
  Harrison glares at himself in the
mirror.

———

He was officially a cliché. A staring at the bathroom mirror, giving himself a pep talk *cliché*. This was a low point.

After they'd changed, Hayley had decided it was too silent, and now the melodic sounds of love songs filtered in from the other room.

Alcohol was tearing down his walls.

It was disastrous. Or bound to be.

Because he'd gone and done the one thing he thought was impossible.

He was more than halfway in love with her, and now he didn't have the slightest clue what to do about it.

Shit.

He'd known what spending this week with her would do. They'd been dancing around it, speaking double for days.

Maybe Hayley was right... maybe it was time to stop running and let himself feel it for a change.

"Don't fuck it up," he said to himself.

"Listen to this review I just found," Hayley said as he returned. "Kyle's script of a woman who spends her time lost —"

Harrison advanced on her.

Hayley jumped back, still reading from her phone's

screen. "— in imagination offers an intriguing commentary on mental health and growing up."

He stalked after her, around the armchair, then the coffee table, always a step behind as she continued.

"A soul-searching tale about generational trauma and the way emotional neglect affects and informs our identities."

Harrison reached for the phone, but she was too quick, her giggles following her as she went on.

"Her obsession with escape has kept her from knowing herself truly, even while she explores the very depths of her own fantasies."

He tried again. She ducked under his arm and jumped over the couch.

"By the time she confronts her parents, she's undergone a journey, becoming a more balanced, if less interesting, individual, but one who finally feels in control of her own destiny." She lowered her phone. "Sounds impressive."

He came to stand in front of her, the barest inch of space left between them. "And yet you still beat me out for best original screenplay."

"You have to admit, that was a pretty good night."

He traced the line of her jaw. "It was."

When her breath hitched, he leaned in, needing to take her lips with his.

"And you've been busy since then," she said, pulling away before he made contact and refilling her wine. She frowned when the bottle was empty. "Travel, work. Dating… I assume."

She was a terrible actress. It was adorable.

"I don't make time for a lot of things. Dating espe-cially. It's never seemed important, and anytime I've tried, it hasn't worked out well. It's nothing like the movies."

"It rarely is," Hayley agreed.

"I'd be lying if I said I'd never felt it. That," he waved a hand, purely to avoid saying the word, then realized he was gesturing between them and stopped. That kind of honesty required at least another glass of wine. Probably a bottle. Then some whiskey. "Magic," he said. "So I know it's not all a lie."

"How magnanimous of you. Have you thought about writing greeting cards?" Her eyes sparkled in the low light, and desire stirred hot in his gut.

"Funny you say that, actually…"

"Let me guess, you wanted to write an award-winning novel, and when that didn't work out, you started slumming it in screenwriting."

"Wow. Tell me what you really think of me."

Hayley's smile faded as she sat, and Harrison worried he'd trampled on another fragile moment.

Great work.

"Sorry, that was harsh."

He shrugged. "I deserved it."

"Maybe a little."

They shared a smile.

He took the seat beside her. "Actually, I used to write radio plays, which then turned into actual plays. Local theater, but nothing to thumb your nose at. After my fourth one, I was approached by a producer wanting to buy the film rights, and there was a bonus attached if I agreed to adapt the screenplay myself. I was rooming with three other guys at the time, and the idea of affording my own place was enough for me to google 'how to write a script' and take the money."

Hayley's expression was caught between amusement and disbelief. "You're joking."

"Nope. True story." Harrison scratched the back of his neck. "I don't usually tell people about that last part."

Hayley mimed locking her lips up. "It stays between us then."

"I don't know. Maybe that's why I fight so hard. I came from nothing. I didn't go to a fancy school — no offense —"

"None taken."

"And I don't want to give anyone the ammo they'd need to question my work."

"You're so talented, Harry. People see that. You should let your guard down. Let us in."

He wanted that, at least right then, in that room, with her. His foolish heart was suited up, bouncing on the diving board, ready to jump, his pulse hammering in his throat.

"Easy to say when your grad short scored one of the most sought-after awards in British film."

Her cheeks flushed bright pink, her mouth opening and closing around air for a few seconds.

Eventually, Harrison saved her from responding.

"You were back there recently, right? For your friend Matt's west end debut."

"I was. How did you…?"

"I saw it on Instagram."

"Keeping tabs on me?"

"Something like that."

"Funny since you don't have any social media that I could find."

"Keeping tabs on me?"

"You're a difficult man to get a hold of. After a month of not hearing from you —"

"I'm sorry about that."

"Are you very mad that you're here?"

"No. I'm…" The words caught in his throat. *About to combust if I don't kiss you* didn't seem appropriate. "I'm not angry," he said in the end, knowing it wasn't enough. "Do you miss the UK?"

"Sometimes, but it hasn't been home in a long time. I have a life here now. Things I want to do."

"People you want to see?"

"Precisely." When she laughed, really laughed, usually at herself, her cheeks would almost hide her eyes. Joy burst from her. She was… beautiful.

She made everything beautiful.

"It's been difficult being so far from my friends, but we message all the time and call when we can. I always knew I'd move away after university, but it doesn't mean I don't get lonely sometimes."

"I can relate. Emilia and I don't go more than a few days without talking. I miss her, but I'm doing exactly what I always wanted, and I know she's happy for me."

"That's how I feel." She leaned closer. "I couldn't imagine being anywhere else right now."

"What else do you want to do?"

"Mmm? You mean in the future?" She looked longingly at her empty glass. "Christ, I don't know. I usually don't think that far ahead."

"I wish I could stop worrying about it. What happens next. What if I've made the wrong choice? Taken a wrong step? I don't miss writing spec, but I'm also sick of writing for other people. Being the guy who rewrites the rewrite wasn't what I was hoping for when I first sold." That first sale had felt incredible. These days, fewer and fewer specs were finding homes, and he wasn't keen on going back to the backbreaking anxiety that came along with it. "That's why I'm here. It's the last obligation on my contract, and then I'm free to write what I want."

"What do you want to do next?"

"Not make a mistake."

He retreated to the minibar, the conversation veering too close to vulnerable for his comfort. It had been far too long since he'd opened up to anyone. Hayley lowered his defenses like no one else.

He pulled out two small bottles of tequila and returned to the couch, holding one out to her. She hesitated briefly, then uncapped the bottle and knocked it back in one go.

Guess he wasn't the only one on edge.

"And just so you know, I haven't seen anyone since that night."

He reached out and brushed the hair off her shoulder, pushing aside the drape of her sweater, watching as goosebumps rippled out across her bare skin.

Even over the sounds of Nat King Cole, Harrison could make out Hayley's sharp intake of breath.

"Dance with me."

Hayley bit her lip, indecision written on her face.

This was probably a bad idea, but he didn't want to listen to reason right now. "What are you afraid of?"

It was the right thing to say. Heat and challenge rose up to meet him, her dark eyes locked on his. "Your two left feet, mostly. I wouldn't want to mess up my pedicure."

"I'll step lightly." He curled his fingers, beckoning her.

Hayley slipped one hand into his, the other dancing along his neck, sparking electricity under his skin. Yep. This was a terrible, fantastic idea.

Her lips looked so much softer up close.

"Do you need me to lead? I know how bad you are with directions," she joked when they hadn't moved.

Damn, he'd gotten lost in her again.

"Only when I don't know where I'm going."

Her lashes fluttered. He spotted a fresh cluster of freckles across her nose, so faint most would probably miss them. They could only be seen from an intimate distance. Practically kissing.

They were his new favorite thing.

He lifted his hand, brushing over them with his thumb. "But I think I'm exactly where I need to be."

She parted her lips and squeezed his hand.

Maybe it was all their talk about romance or the music they were swaying to. Really, it was how perfectly she fit into him, chest to chest, her nose tucked into his neck.

He never had a chance to keep the words back. "Sometimes you're so beautiful it's almost hard to look at you." His lips brushed her ear. "Let me kiss you?"

She nodded shakily.

He leaned in, kissing her neck, tugging the collar of her sweater to taste the dip of her collarbone, her shoulder.

Her grip tightened as he continued to avoid her lips. "Harry, please."

He smiled against her skin. "I want more than one night with you, Hayley. I want more than I probably deserve."

"I want it, too."

He raised his head, locked on to her darkening eyes, and finally pressed his mouth to hers.

She responded instantly, opening under him as sweetly as he remembered, the tang of tequila sharp on her tongue. Free to act on every urge he'd had in the last few days, he took charge, hand in her hair, kissing her with abandon.

God, he'd almost forgotten the hungry little sounds she made.

He couldn't stop himself from returning to her neck, nipping and sucking as Hayley cupped the back of his head, holding him in place.

As if he was going anywhere.

Slipping his hands under her sweater, he said, "I'm going to tear your clothes off now, so if you want to stop me, you better be quick."

"Shut up and do it already."

Nimble fingers were already at his belt. He captured her lips again, kissing her while he pulled her shirt up, not caring that he was delaying his own damn plan. She tasted too good. How had he gone the week without it?

There was a hiss of a zipper and the rustle of clothing hitting the floor, but it wasn't until Hayley abruptly pulled away from him to pull her shirt over her head that he realized she'd abandoned his pants in favor of removing her own. Suddenly, she stood before him in black lingerie. Not thin lace, like he'd expected.

No, her body was adorned with thick straps and buckles, and good fucking god, he might have to find some way of fucking her without removing them because how could he mess with art like this?

"Harry."

He blinked. She was indescribable. Every place his eyes landed was better than the last. Soft, luscious thighs, but also her calves. Never had he wanted to worship someone's calves before, but right now, he could happily sink to his knees and pay them the attention they deserved. Follow them with his hands and his mouth, up those incredible thighs to her hips… Fuck, he hardly knew where to start. It didn't matter. He wanted his tongue everywhere. Where her thigh met her ass, the dip of her pelvis, along the high V of her panties, all the way down to her sweet pussy.

"Harry."

Not that he'd stop there. He could live between her thighs. Subsist on her juices alone. He'd been thinking about it for days. He wouldn't even have to remove the underwear; he could get her on her side and —

"Harry! For Christ's sake, will you stop drooling and kiss me already?"

With a sound deep in his throat, he stalked toward her, crashing his mouth against hers. Lips met teeth and tongue.

Her thighs fit as perfectly as she remembered in his palms, and in seconds, he'd tugged her up, legs around his waist. He moved them back to the bedroom.

"I wanted to get you naked."

Her voice broke. "You were taking too long."

"You are so fucking sexy," he said, tonguing the cup of her bra.

She jumped down once they were in the bedroom, stripping him of his sweater and pants while he fished the condom out of his back pocket. Down to his boxers now, he hooked a hand in her hair to kiss her again.

Hayley scratched her nails through the light scruff around his nipples before giving him one hard push, and he let himself fall back onto the bed, hands behind his head.

Hayley removed her lingerie, and Harrison missed them for a half of a second.

Jesus. Fucking. Christ.

Had he called her art before?

She was a fucking goddess.

His boxers strained, a wet patch growing as he hardened and leaked. The right kind of friction, and he'd be done. The kicker, though, was seeing Hayley as caught up in him as he was in her. Damn if the look she was giving him right now didn't make him feel like *GQ*'s man of the year.

She licked her lips, and his dick jumped, bobbing its approval. He palmed it, enjoying the way her blush spread across her neck and chest while she watched. He imagined the pulse of wetness between her thighs. God, those thighs…

Hayley placed her hands on the bed, one on either side of his waist, then leaned in to suck him through the thin cotton.

Harrison threw his head back, groaning. Shit, he was close already.

Thankfully, she didn't linger. There was no way Harrison could edge tonight. There'd hopefully be plenty of time for that later. After she'd removed his boxers, he caught her wrist and pulled her up to straddle him, kissing her long and deep, enjoying the way his dick nestled between her cheeks.

She slid her fingers up his arms, and he let her have this moment, content to lie back. She plucked the condom from his fingers, then pulled back to sit on his thighs.

"I want to go bare," she said, and he almost forgot to breathe. "Have you been tested?"

"Yeah, last month. All good," he said, still wrapping his mind around the fact that she wanted him bare.

"Same, and the implant is still in," she said. "So…" She held the little packet out, offering Harrison the choice.

He snatched it from between her fingers and threw it onto the floor. Lifting himself to his elbows, he pulled her in, licking into her mouth as he thrust against her. Her moans tasted so sweet. The movement let his dick slip between her, slick with arousal. She was dripping. The room smelled like sex already.

Could he make her squirt?

Maybe he'd try tomorrow. In the shower, up against the wall, on his knees. Her clit between his lips, and his fingers hitting just the right angle until she gushed.

Hayley bit down on his bottom lip, pulling him back to reality. Gripping the globes of her ass in his hands, he reached farther, teasing the sensitive skin between them all the way to her hole. She gasped, exposing her neck, and Harrison took advantage, licking and sucking a series of bruises into the skin.

Hayley raked her nails over his back and shoulders as he writhed. She tried to move, sink down, but Harrison kept her where she was, teasing her with his fingers. The head of his dick was trapped between them, sliding between her soaked lips to graze her clit. Then, his hands on her hips, he shifted, lining himself up and hauling her down onto his cock.

Heat engulfed him.

Above him, Hayley let out a whimpered sigh, the broken sound loud in his ears.

He kept his hands gripping her hips as he fell back against the bed, groaning. "You feel incredible. Why haven't we been doing this all week?"

Hayley rolled her hips, pulling moans from them both. "Don't blame me, you're the one who — yes, Harry, right there — couldn't take a hint."

She sighed, and all the air was stolen from Harrison's lungs. She was gorgeous, eyes alight and burning into him — her whole body was white hot, her thighs hugging his hips, her pussy gripping his cock, the heat of her mouth as he licked inside. He hadn't forgotten how good it had been last time, fast and heaving against the back wall of a closet, the scent of cologne and cigarettes wafting off the coats around them. But this, Hayley rocking against him, their kisses wet and filthy, the promise of *more* — all the ways he could fuck those sounds out of her — was infinitely better.

"Yes." Harrison thrust, his hands tight on her waist, caught in the feel of her moving above him, the way she used him to chase her own pleasure. How her breath caught when he cupped her breasts, raising up to his elbows so he could lick and suck and mark up the tender skin.

Words failed him — as a writer he should be ashamed — but how could he think properly with her straddling him, her back arched, dark nipples peaked under his fingers, panting as she rode him?

When her rhythm faulted, he pulled into his reserves to really fuck into her. Hard and fast. No time to think about finesse, because she was gasping, nails almost painfully tight on his shoulders, her pussy throbbing around him as she came.

His own orgasm thundered through him.

She panted as she fell onto the bed beside him, rolling over to rest her head on his arm. "Fuck, Harry."

He couldn't think of a better way of putting it.

Groaning, she rolled off the bed and walked to the bathroom to clean up, the sight of her bare back and stunning ass giving Harrison's dick ideas it had no way of making good on, at least not for another half hour.

Harrison stared at the ceiling, willed his heart to stop racing, and knew he was too far gone to pretend otherwise.

"You haven't fallen asleep on me, have you?" Hayley fit easily into his side, pulling the sheet over them.

Ridiculous turns of phrase filtered through his thoughts, words he'd be embarrassed to type but would probably fit perfectly among the lines of their script.

He traced the dip and curve of her spine. "Would that be a crime? You've worn me out."

She slipped her leg over his before letting out a deep yawn. "As long as you're not ruined. I have plans for tomorrow."

"I'm not ruined." *Yet.*

As her breathing evened out, he placed a gentle kiss to her temple, tasting the lingering sweat there.

Of all the lies he'd ever told, that one was probably the most egregious. Of course she had. From the moment they'd met, her teasing barbs, astute glare, and incredible mind had set him on a path to disaster. And he'd gone willingly.

As sleep overtook him, Harrison recognized exactly how bad things had become.

Because if his life had turned into a movie, what were the chances that he'd get his happily ever after?

Friday

39 INT. HOTEL — BEDROOM — DAY

Harrison's face. PULL BACK and they are tangled together, naked.

———

Before he even opened his eyes, Harrison rocked forward, pulling Hayley closer, needing more of her heat and the perfect curve of her ass. Perfectly content, he hummed, burying his nose in her hair and breathing her in as deeply as he could. His dick was a heavy weight, hard and ready. The list he'd been compiling sprung to the forefront of his mind.

Slowly, he blinked, hearing the change in her breathing as she stirred. He brushed the hair from her shoulder, kissing along her neck, bathing in the way her breath hitched and stuttered, how she stretched against him, head falling back, asking for more.

He followed the line of her hipbone, sliding his hand between her legs, finding her wet and waiting. Fuck. He wouldn't ever get enough of her.

It had been ridiculous, really, thinking he could have escaped the intensity of his emotions. Holding her, her skin hot under his lips, her body fitting so perfectly under his hands, it set his hopes alight with possibility.

He had no idea what this meant to Hayley, but what he felt for her wasn't fleeting or casual. He wouldn't repeat the same mistake as last time.

If he had any luck at all, she would let him spend the rest of his life making it up to her.

Maybe he could call for breakfast. And hopefully grow a new personality before it arrived. Convince her to give him a chance.

Yeah, sure.

But before he could suggest food, she sneezed. And before he could say anything, it happened again.

"Oh, no," she said, her voice raw. Had that happened overnight?

He pulled his hand back, concerned. "Are you cold?"

"I'm sick," she said, turning to him. And boy, she looked it. Bloodshot eyes, pallid skin. He hadn't seen anyone get so sick so fast before.

"It happens every time I drink tequila. Something about the fermentation process kicks off an allergy. I can't remember."

"Why didn't you say anything? I would've chosen something else." He felt terrible.

"I was hoping I'd get lucky." Even through the puffiness, she winked. "Guess I was right."

Harrison softly laughed. She was so perfectly ridiculous. He might need to marry her.

He pulled back when she reached for him. She frowned, looking as disappointed as his dick felt. "Okay, sex machine. How about you lie back down. You need to rest."

"I can't," she said, pushing his hands away as he tried to pull the duvet over her. "We have to work."

"You can't work; you're sick."

"I'm fine."

Like hell she was. She sounded like an octogenarian

with an iron lung. Her body succumbed to another round of coughs.

"Really. This is you fine?"

She nodded after one last bark. "Yes," she wheezed out. "Now leave me alone."

"Not a chance."

She begged him off. "You'll get sick."

He scoffed. "You said I had no feelings, right? There's not enough here for germs to want me," he joked, but stopped short at the wide-eyed fondness in Hayley's gaze. Even puffy and shot through with red, her eyes had the power to undo him. "Come on, lie back. I saw a pharmacy a couple of blocks over. I'll run out and grab you some drugs."

"I always did fall for the bad boys," she said, and Harrison winced at how raw and rough her voice was.

He walked across the room and dialed room service. "Yeah, can I get a pot of Earl Grey up to the honeymoon suite? Thanks."

When he turned back, Hayley was staring at him. Even with a red nose and bloodshot eyes, the force of her warm gaze hit Harrison directly.

"My hero."

————

The nearest pharmacy was two blocks away. It had been a while since Harrison had gotten sick, which was a miracle considering how much he traveled, and while Hayley had been insistent that it wasn't like the flu, it sure had all the symptoms of one, so he figured buying whatever flu medicine he could find couldn't hurt.

And okay, maybe he went slightly overboard, throwing in three different brands of antihistamine and a pain reliever with *drowsy* and *15% more effective* written on the label. Just to be safe, he added a few bottles of juice, lozenges, a vapor rub that promised to clear airways, tissues, chocolate, ice cream, and a heating pad.

He had probably gone overboard, but by the time he stopped second-guessing himself, he was walking into the lobby of the hotel.

"Mr. Kyle?"

Harrison stopped in his tracks. A few days ago, he'd been ready to demand the hotel manager fix their sleeping arrangements, but today the man was the last person he wanted to see.

"Yes? Is there something wrong?" What else could possibly happen? Had they built an additional floor in the last forty-eight hours? Would he and Hayley be moved up to some sprawling penthouse, complete with a cherub fountain entryway and butler?

"I called up to the room, but there was no answer. I wanted to let Ms. Bennett know that her previous room has been vacated. We'd be happy to move her back in if she wishes."

Well, *damn.* Not the news Harrison had been hoping for. It wasn't his place to answer for Hayley, and neither of them had been keen on sharing a room, but now he was feeling selfish. He wanted to keep her with him.

He should say no. Hayley was sick, and it was only a

few more days. But his damn conscience wouldn't let him. Clearly, she was having a bad influence. He sighed.

"Hold the room for her, and I'll let you know."

If Hayley needed her space while she was sick, he wouldn't make her move. Better for her to take the suite. She could relax and recuperate there, and Harrison would go.

———

Juggling multiple bags while attempting to fish the key card out of his pocket was an experience he hoped to never repeat. Somewhere in the hotel, there was no doubt a security guy watching him on a screen and judging him.

When he finally got into the room, he registered familiar voices. The mystery was solved when he entered the bedroom to find his phone set to speaker on the bedside table and Hayley sitting up against the headboard, happily chatting to it.

"Oh, Harry you're back. Your sister called. At first, I let it go to voice mail —"

Emilia cut in, her voice playful. "And then I texted to say that if you didn't answer, I was going to post your pirate dance to TikTok."

"And I knew I had to save you from such a fate."

Harrison had known this would happen. Already, they were peas in a pod. He was doomed.

"You showed her, didn't you?" he asked, already knowing the answer.

Hayley beamed. "It's very cute, Harry. I didn't know you could tap dance."

Completely and utterly doomed.

"Where were you anyway?" Emilia asked. "Don't you know your girl is sick? Your bedside manner needs work, brother."

"My bedside manner is none of your business. And I was out getting supplies, thank you very much." He placed the bags on the bed. As Hayley rifled through their contents, he took his phone off speaker to talk to Emilia directly. "What's the emergency? Is everything okay at work?"

As a case manager for a youth social work program, Emilia often had her hands full, but Harrison couldn't think of a person more suited for it. She'd been his protective big sister growing up — hell, she still fulfilled that role — and now she dedicated her days to helping as many kids as she could.

Whenever he worried that he lacked the capacity to love, he thought about Emilia, and he knew what it was to care for someone with your whole heart.

"No emergency. I wanted to find out how things were going. Imagine my surprise when Hayley mentioned you'd left your phone by the bed."

Harrison groaned internally. He'd known this was coming but had hoped he wouldn't have to deal with it until after he'd left Chance.

"I take it you didn't quit yesterday."

From his spot at the doorway, he spared a glance at the bed, where Hayley was throwing back some pills with juice. He moved into the living room. "No, I didn't.

And before you ask, yes, something happened. No, I can't talk about it. And yes, I'll tell you everything when I get home on Sunday."

"She's funny. I can see what you like about her."

Something meaningful swooped within the confines of his chest, pleased. He should never have doubted it, but having Emilia's approval loosened the tension in his shoulders. "It's so much more than that. She's..." He barely knew where to start.

"When do I get to meet her?" Emilia asked, putting into words something he had been afraid of wanting. What if this was an anomaly? There was no denying that he and Hayley had chemistry, but did that mean she'd want to have anything to do with him after this week?

She might be in the other room counting down the days until she was rid of him.

"You'd tell me if I was making a mistake," he said, the question obvious. He found himself biting at his nails. "I should never have let Lee talk me into this," he said, then remembered Hayley's confession last night. That she had asked to work with him. Maybe it wasn't ridiculous to think she might feel something for him.

It didn't stop him from worrying, though.

"You're not, I promise you. Please don't stop yourself from going after this. I know you hate being vulnerable and all that, but I really think Hayley's one of the good ones."

"You talked to her for five minutes. You can't possibly know that."

"That's all it took," Emilia said.

Harrison couldn't even argue with her. He was pretty certain it hadn't even taken him that long.

––––––

Harrison laughed at the text from Emilia. "My sister just said that she's keeping you if things don't work out, FYI."

"Good. I don't plan on going anywhere." Her smile morphed into a cough, and she grimaced. "Of course, it's going to be hard when Olsen fires me after we miss the deadline."

He placed a hand on her knee. "It'll be fine. We're so close to finishing, We've got what? Fifteen pages left? That's nothing."

"It's just the big ending; no need to worry." Only Hayley could master sarcasm while sick.

"We'll figure it out. I'll tell them it's my fault. I dragged my feet for too long, and we ran out of time."

"No, you can't say that."

"Why not? It's the truth."

"Harry. No." She sniffled, then yawned. "Whatever we tell them, we face it together."

The suite's doorbell rang. "That'll be your tea," he said, kissing her cheek.

––––––

"I hate being sick," Hayley said, bringing a tissue to her face, then sneezing into it. She'd complained loudly enough about being bedridden that they'd moved into the living area, blankets and all. "I must look disgusting."

"You don't."

Hayley glared at him. Or attempted to. Her eyes were so red and puffy they were practically closed.

He pulled a strand of sweat-soaked hair from her temple. "I'm not lying. You're beautiful."

"Stop trying to make me feel better." Another sneeze.

He chuckled. "Okay, I'll stop. But only because you asked me to." He passed her another Kleenex, softly adding, "It doesn't change how I feel."

"You're impossible," she attempted to say.

Harrison had to laugh at how she sounded, her stuffy nose rendering her words unintelligible. Within seconds, they were both laughing, although Hayley had to stop to cough halfway through.

Harrison was quick to pick her feet up off the floor, forcing her to make herself comfortable on the couch while he draped her with a thick blanket.

"I wouldn't have guessed you to have such a good bedside manner," she said, snuggling under the blanket until she burrowed underneath.

Rubbing her feet over the covers, he said, "Do you want me to go? I can visit our friend down at reception and see if they've freed up another room." He still hadn't told her about the vacancy. He needed to get a feel for what she wanted first. Hopefully it wouldn't bite him in the ass later. "Maybe I'll get lucky, and he'll tell me I won a romantic getaway."

With a weak kick, she shook her head. "Please stay."

He settled back against the couch, toeing his shoes off and reaching for the remote. Once they'd finally agreed on a movie — which was more like Harrison agreeing to whatever Hayley wanted to watch — he reached under the blanket and worked the knots out of her feet, only complaining half as much about the trite holiday romance as he wanted to.

Hayley smiled each time he did, and Harrison found it easier than he thought it would be to enjoy himself.

"You're better than these films, you know."

She interrupted him. "Not again. Harry, just say you're a snob and move on. It's much quicker."

"Seriously," he had to say it. "You're an amazing writer. You could be doing —"

"What? Real movies?" she asked, but there was no heat behind it.

"You know what I meant."

She sniffled, then exhaled a deep sigh. "Of course I question it. I know it isn't," she lifted one hand to weakly mimic air quotes, "*art*. But I care about the stories I write. They make people happy. They make me happy."

He stilled, feeling the delicate bones of her ankle under his fingers. "I was wrong the other day. Writing these isn't as easy as I thought. Harder, actually." Everything about this week had been more difficult than he'd expected, but he didn't regret a second of it. Even now, surrounded by tissues and Hayley's soft wheezing breaths, he was happier than he could remember being in a long time.

And it was all thanks to her.

"I told you not to bet against me," she rasped. "Now you're two for two."

He was a hell of a lot more behind than that.

———

Hayley was in the shower when Lee called, and Harrison was busy strategizing an exit.

"Ready to quit?" Lee joked.

But Harrison wasn't joking. "I think I should." Sure, it was for a completely different set of reasons than yesterday — and it had not escaped Harrison's notice how little time had passed — but it was the right thing. He could handle working with the studio a little longer if it meant she got the recognition she deserved.

"Whoa, what? You're serious."

"Deadly. Tell them I'll write whatever they want."

"Uh, you might want to hold that thought. There was something I didn't you about this whole deal. Hayley's contract is on the chopping block. The only reason they allowed her to pick a co-writer was because it was you. Look, I don't know how they knew, but they set you both up to fail."

The fuck? "Tell me you're joking."

"I wish I could. They want to cut her loose, man. It's bullshit, but it's true. Why do you think I pushed you to stay?"

"Why didn't you tell me this earlier?"

"Because I was afraid you'd tell her."

"Damn right I would have. This is complete fucking bullshit."

"You don't have to tell me. I'm trying to help both of you here."

Fuck. He didn't even know where to start. Pacing seemed as good a place as any. Self-loathing a close second. He'd almost eaten right from their hand.

"That's why I called. They want the first draft by morning."

"What? That doesn't make sense. Even if I send it right now, they won't have time to read it by tomorrow. It's an arbitrary deadline. They gave us a week."

"Exactly. They want to prove that you couldn't work together. By pushing up the timeline —"

Hayley shuffled back into the room.

"Yeah, yeah, I know. Okay," Harrison said, catching Hayley's fond smile as she joined him. "Don't worry, we'll get it done."

"Sounds like it's going well with you two." And oh god, his voice had turned smug again. The last time it did that, Harrison had ended up in this mess. "What's this I hear about a honeymoon suite?"

"Such a shame I'm going through a tunnel right now," Harrison said, just catching Lee's "asshole" through the phone before he hung up.

"What's wrong?" Hayley asked.

"The studio needs a draft by tomorrow." He scrubbed at his face with both hands. "I should call him back and tell him we won't make it."

"What are you," she paused to yawn, "talking about? The drugs shouldn't kick in for at least an hour. Let's get through as much as we can."

"Are you sure? You look pretty tired."

"I thought you said I looked beautiful."

"You do, and stop changing the subject. Are you feeling up to this?"

Hayley grabbed him by the shirt, pulling him in with a surprising amount of strength, considering she was struggling to stay upright. "Yes. Are you?"

He fought back a smile, worried she'd find the strength to kick him in the dick if he laughed at how adorable she was. And he liked his dick. He planned on using it again at some point, hopefully with her. He nodded.

"Great. So we're both good."

A chuckle escaped him, and he pulled back just as she whacked his shoulder.

"Stop laughing and get in here. We have work to do."

"Yes, dear."

The problem with drowsy medication, it turned out, was how effective it was. Within minutes, Hayley could barely keep her eyes open, but she fought through the exhaustion.

"And we should use your idea of the, um, the thing, at the end, because that was a good idea. Which you're full of. Do you know I haven't felt this engaged in my work in years? That's why I wanted you. Well," the word was lost in a long yawn. "And because I wanted to see you again. I missed you."

It was a good thing her eyes were closed, because Harrison was fairly certain his heart was beating on the outside of his chest. If he gave it a pen, he was sure it would be writing their initials on itself and circling them.

"Don't disappear this time, okay?" she murmured.

With a lapful of sleeping beauty, Harrison abandoned the script, pushing their notes to the side so he could wrap the blanket more comfortably around Hayley's shoulders.

He wasn't going anywhere. Not this time.

He sat in silence, enjoying her steady weight against him, the rhythm of her breathing. Baby hairs were plastered to her forehead, her skin still holding a faint clamminess, and he brushed them back. Would she be too warm like this? Maybe he should move her to the bed. That had to be more comfortable than sleeping on him.

His phone beeped loudly, signaling a message, and he silenced it before reading. Emilia was checking in on Hayley. With one arm still trapped around her shoulders, he took a selfie of the two of them curled up on the couch and sent it back to his sister. Her response was a series of hearts.

It was hard to take a full breath. His lungs squeezed like he'd eaten too much, and his heart was too big for his chest. Maybe he had indigestion. Maybe it was a heart attack.

It would be just his luck for his heart to give out on him just as he was finally using it.

Every once in a while, Hayley stirred, murmuring quietly in her sleep, while Harrison continued to run his fingers through her hair. She really was beautiful. It didn't matter that her nose was puffy and red, the blocked airways making her snore a little. It wouldn't even matter if she looked nothing like she did. Yes, he was physically attracted to her, sometimes so much it amazed him that he'd managed to get any work done this week, but fuck, it was so much more than that.

He'd meant what he said to Emilia. When he pictured the future, this was what he wanted.

As the realization hit home, he stilled. He couldn't move, could barely breathe for the force of it. The weight of knowing that for the rest of his life, he would love her. This incredible human who could walk away, hurt, judge, scorn, disappoint, lie.

He could imagine just about anything, but the idea of Hayley — someone so genuine, so dedicated — being malicious… it was unfathomable.

Loving Emilia had always been easy. Loving his job, his writing, was natural. Like waking up, or blinking.

Loving Hayley felt inevitable. Like a purpose. Not to be wasted or treated lightly. But worked toward, reclaimed through action every day.

As often as he could.

———

Hayley barely stirred when he moved her to the bedroom and tucked her under the sheets. He made sure everything she might need was within reach. Their clothes still littered the floor from last night. Even the sight of them brought back every touch. As he picked up his pants, the flower she'd adorned him with fell to the floor. Had it really only been a day since then?

Everything about this week had been surreal, like a dream he didn't want to wake up from.

But he would wake up. That was how reality worked. Happily ever afters only occurred in fiction because life didn't end after "I love you." Real life was messy and complicated and wonderful.

And god help him, he wanted it all. But what did Hayley want? What would be waiting for them once this week — and whatever strange spell they were under — was over? And it would be over. He couldn't expect anything more. Not without serving his heart up on a platter.

With a gentle kiss to her forehead, he placed the flower by her bedside before closing the door.

46 INT. HOTEL — LOUNGE - NIGHT

———

Harrison scrubbed both hands down his face. He could do this.

With his notes spread out on the floor, he opened their current draft. They'd alternated scenes, and while they'd outlined everything, they had argued over the final moments. Hayley wanted what she referred to as the big "break up and chase down" moment. Harrison had rallied for something a little less over the top.

Now, his fingers poised above the keys, he had a choice to make. Write his version and risk Hayley being mad tomorrow. Or write hers. Somehow. Was he even capable of creating a "chase down" without it coming across as completely saccharine and uninspired?

Why had he ever thought writing romance was easy?

Everyone knew the tropes, the clichés. Boy meets girl, boy loses girl, boy gets girl. Simple.

Harrison wanted to cuff himself upside the head for ever looking down his nose at it. Yes, there were plenty of examples of lazy writing in romance, but no more than in any other genre. And Hayley was absolutely *not* lazy.

She cared about the stories she created and the characters within them. But more than that, she cared about her audience. It wasn't solely about scene beats and emotional arcs; she wanted every single person who watched the film to feel something. Hope. Joy. Love.

Harrison started typing. With every word, his confidence grew, his fingers flying across the keyboard feverishly.

Saturday

ayley's side of the bed was empty when he woke. He tamped down his disappointment. There were any number of reasons she would be up. But he couldn't hear the shower, or the television, and he still had to find a way of explaining what had happened with the script yesterday.

If she heard it from anyone else…

Suddenly, his heart was in his throat. What if she'd already seen it and hated it? He'd assumed she'd forgive him because of the consequences of not meeting the deadline, but now he wasn't so sure. He'd gone behind her back. Yes, she'd been sick at the time, and he'd used her ending, but that didn't give him the right to send it without her approval.

Christ, what if the studio hated it and had already fired her?

Incredible, life-changing moments hardly ever happened to Harrison.

As he reached out and felt the cool touch of her side of the bed, he had the sinking feeling that this particular dream was over.

The script was done, and maybe Hayley was done, too.

H arrison hated this part. Formulaic bullshit was how he'd described it to Hayley.

It was ridiculous.

He refused to fall for it.

Was he really supposed to run around looking for her, chase her down like a lovelorn cliché of a character, ready to declare how he felt to a group of slow clapping extras?

———

48 INT. HOTEL — DAY

He tried their meeting room first.

It had been returned to its original state, not a Post-it in sight. When a chill ran through his chest, he knew the air conditioning wasn't to blame.

For once, he was relieved to find the hotel manager at the front desk. "I'm sorry. She did come by to collect what was left in the meeting room, but she didn't say where she was going."

Of course she hadn't. That would be too easy.

He braved the coffee shop on the corner, but she wasn't there either. She could be anywhere. Had he even seen her suitcase in the room? Fuck.

Lee was his next step.

"Yeah, I spoke with her earlier. She was not happy to find out that you'd sent it in without her."

Shit. "What else did she say?"

"She was pretty pissed at the studio. Said she needed to check her contract and wanted to know if I'd be willing to take a look."

"Wait, you told her about that?"

"She had some choice words to say about you, too."

Shit, shit, shit. Harrison owed her a truck full of flowers. And chocolates. And maybe a lifetime of groveling.

Lee continued, "I explained that you were trying to protect her, even sent her the script so she could see you hadn't cut her out. I have to say, man, I'm impressed. You two make a good team."

"Did she say anything about leaving?"

"Ah, shit. Yeah, she was packing when I called. I'm really sorry."

So that was that.

What could he do? He'd wasted his chance to ask her to stay, tell her how he felt, and now she'd left him the way he'd left her six months ago. Which he deserved.

Festival posters taunted him on the walk back. He had half a mind to run over and see if she'd gone back to Charlie's display, but there was only so much humiliation he could take. She'd left, and there was nothing he could do.

The worst part — the bit that really stung — was that he thought he had more time. He didn't even have her phone number. Emilia was going to have a field day when she found out. What kind of man would fall in love with someone he couldn't contact?

The same pop song played as he rode the elevator to

his room, defeated. Now that the script had been delivered, he probably should check out and make his way home, but he didn't have the energy. A day of wallowing, and then he would scrape what was left of himself together and accept his fate.

He'd found someone worth holding on to, and he'd ruined it with his pessimism and stubbornness, too convinced he'd mess it up to even give it a shot. He could kick himself.

All he wanted was one more chance. The opportunity to tell her how he felt, to ask if she could ever feel the same.

When he exited to find Hayley in the hallway, suitcase in hand, he stopped short. "You're still here."

Her expression was unreadable. Not angry, which was hopefully a good sign. "I'd gone out for tea when Lee called, and then I needed some time to think."

He nodded, his mouth dry. Everything he wanted to say lodged in his throat.

"Lee sent me the script," she said softy.

"I'm sorry," he blurted out. "I should have told you, but I was so angry at the studio, and you'd fallen asleep. It's not a good excuse, and I was going to tell you this morning, but I couldn't find you, and I thought…"

Hayley closed her eyes, shaking her head. "You really are impossible."

"Are you angry about the script?"

Hayley blinked, speaking slowly. "No, Harry, I'm not."

She started to move, but Harrison couldn't take it.

Before she could take a single step, he'd reached out and pulled the suitcase out of her grip.

"Harry, what are you doing?"

"You're not going to run off before I tell you this, because I've seen the chase happen in too many movies, and I don't think I could take living through it."

Hayley opened her mouth, but he didn't wait.

He'd avoided this his whole life. Never thought he'd find it, never wanted it to find him. But he'd be damned if he let it slip through his fingers now.

"Don't leave. I know you're angry with me about the script, and the studio, and probably a million other reasons, which I completely deserve, but I'm asking you, begging actually, to stay."

"Harry, what are you talking about?"

"Your suitcase."

"I was moving back to my room."

"Oh."

The corner of her mouth slid into a teasing smile. "Yes, oh. But please, keep going."

How had he ever thought he could accept life without her?

She was an anchor point, the rewarding calm of his first cup of coffee, the infinite possibility of a blank page, the satisfying conclusion to a problem no one had ever solved.

He cupped her cheek, admiring, let her easy and familiar calm take hold even as his heart beat rapidly in his chest.

"Where should I start?"

"The beginning usually works."

"I've been wrong so many times in my life, but walking away from you six months ago was the stupidest thing I've ever done. I won't make that mistake again. There's no good excuse, except to say that I was afraid. How I feel about you is terrifying and incredible, and I didn't know how to deal with it, so I ran. And when you walked into that room, I panicked."

He had so much to make up for. Months of moments they'd never get back, with only the hope that she'd give him the chance to do it right.

"I couldn't let myself believe that this would end happily, because those endings never felt possible for me. But I kept wanting it — wanting you — and I planned to tell you this yesterday, but then Lee called, and then you were gone this morning and —"

Hayley cut him off with a kiss.

"Honestly. I've only been waiting for you to say something. You're not the only one who couldn't stay away, Harry. I've been telling myself for months to get over you, that what we had was a temporary thing. But I kept thinking about you, and I had to know —"

He couldn't hold himself back any longer. He slid his arm around her waist and kissed her. It was hard to hold back, on anything — his relief that she hadn't left, the pleasure of hearing that she felt the same, the adrenaline rush of what tomorrow might bring. He didn't want to back away from it any longer, so he let it flow through him, translated it into every press of his lips, the curl of his tongue, feeling it returned as Hayley hummed happy little sounds and pulled at his shirt.

It left him lightheaded. "I should have done that the minute I saw you."

Hayley ducked her head. Her hair fanned across her cheeks, but it couldn't hide the blush.

And god help him, but he finally got it. Everything she'd been saying. If he could use his words to make another person feel the way he did right now — blood singing, chest bursting with love — wasn't he duty bound to do it? Disappointment, frustration, boredom couldn't be avoided, not forever. But hope, joy, love were to be coveted, shared.

He brushed the high point of her cheek with his lips. "I…"

Hayley pressed closer, capturing his mouth, pulling him by the neck, as he gathered her closer, arms tight around her back.

"It's okay. You don't have to say it."

But he did.

He wanted to.

What he felt for her was momentous. It couldn't really be as simple as a few words, could it? He needed to go big, express it in a way that befit the enormity of his love for her. It was silly, but she'd been calling him that since they met, no reason to dissuade her from the truth now. If she minded, she wouldn't be here, right? So why not embrace it? It was only what she'd been trying to get him to do since the start of the week. Emilia would be proud. Harrison might have been the last person to get it, but better late than never.

The hallway was too small, too blank, too bright. He couldn't tell her here. What kind of writer was he?

"I wanna do this right."

"Did you do it wrong the other night? Because I'm happy to help you practice."

Fuck. He wanted to get wrecked in the best way.

"No, I mean, this." He gestured weakly, distracted as she bit his jaw and palmed his cock.

"Harry?"

"Hold that thought. Can we go somewhere?"

Confusion settled between her brows, but Hayley nodded.

49 EXT. COURTYARD - DAY

———

"Explain to me why we had to come here," Hayley said, but there was no hiding her smile, so he was 80 percent sure he couldn't fuck this up.

They'd returned to the courtyard. He'd considered the festival, but having that many witnesses was pushing it. With the way his blood was rushing in his ears, he wasn't entirely sure he'd make it through his impromptu speech without passing out.

"Because I need to say this."

And surprisingly, he wasn't as afraid as he thought he'd be. He'd spent so much time picturing this moment with a sick feeling, but it was easy. Loving her came naturally to him.

Hayley's eyes darted around quickly, a flash of panic he'd never seen before crossing her face. "You're not about to start dancing, are you?"

Laughter bubbled out of him, breaking through the tension. This is why they were perfect together. "No."

"Thank goodness."

He held her hands in his, relieved that he wasn't the only one trembling. No one ever mentioned how fucking scary this was.

"Life isn't a movie. Sometimes bad things happen. One of us will mess up — probably me, let's be honest — but I don't care about any of that. Because when I'm with you, I don't want to be anywhere else. Good or bad, I want to experience it all, as long as you're with me."

Her eyes sparkled, the sun's glow holding her gently in its light. He took a deep breath. He was a writer with a flair for dramatics; of course he could do this. He'd give her the best damn speech she'd ever heard.

Or he'd embarrass himself and never be able to show his face again, becoming a reclusive writer haunted by his own past, like the protagonist of a made for TV thriller... but either way, it would be memorable.

It would certainly make a good story to tell their grandkids someday.

"The thought of not seeing you tomorrow or the day after that is painful to me. Every minute I spend not kissing you, I feel like I'm going to die. And this probably isn't the speech you've dreamed of, but if you let me, I will spend our lives rewriting it."

Hayley curled her fingers around his, a lifeline.

"You've spent all week telling me to stop over-thinking it. To feel. And shit, I have no idea what I'm doing, but I know I can do that, because since the day I met you, I've done nothing but feel. I can't stop. You only need to walk into a room, and I'm done for. I want the happily ever after, and I'll embrace every cheesy cliché there is if it means even one extra minute with you."

Harrison willed his pulse to slow. He only needed to get through the next few terrifying minutes, and then he could think about having a heart attack.

"I'm in love with you. I can't let you leave without

telling you that. The only thing I need to know now is how you feel."

A myriad of emotions played over her features, but her eyes never strayed from his. Once, twice, her mouth opened and shut, words aborted before they could form.

"Harry," she said, the sound breaking halfway. "You really should have warned me. I could have written something in advance. Of course I love you."

"Say it again."

"I love you," she said, beaming. "Don't you believe me?"

"I do, even if I don't understand it. I'm messy and bitter and opinionated."

"Nobody's perfect," she joked.

"You are."

She snorted. "I'm the furthest thing from perfect, and you know it. But that's why we work so well together."

"You're not thinking clearly. All this romance is clouding your mind."

It didn't matter that they were outside, in the middle of this courtyard, where anyone could see him make a fool of himself. For her, he'd do anything, even if he knew Lee and Emilia would never let him live this moment down.

Hayley slid her a hand around his neck, her touch gentle, reassuring.

"I'm not going anywhere, you know. And I don't want you any other way."

"Really?"

Hayley only smiled, her eyes glittering.

He slid his free hand into her hair, the strands silky and soft. "You're sure there's not a single other way you want me?"

"I guess I could think of a few more, if pressed."

"What if we fight?"

"Then we'll make up. Repeatedly." She leaned in, whispering, "I can be very creative."

"I want to prove that we're good together. I want to make this work." He couldn't bear to pull back. Skimming her cheek with his lips, he reveled in the rise and fall of her chest against his, the soft fall of her breath against his neck. "It takes what, ten thousand hours to master something?"

Her eyes, sparkling honey brown in the sunlight, never left his.

"So let me try. Give me ten thousand hours to prove my love to you."

"Harry…" A breath, a laugh, a promise. Hayley pressed it against his lips, soft and sure. "That's a long time. We should get started as soon as possible."

It was difficult to kiss while smiling as hard as he was, but he was up for the challenge. Now sounded good. Perfect. Spectacular.

"Whatever you want."

Hayley shook her head, laughing. "You're full of surprises."

———

Nearby, a street performer pulled out a guitar and sang, garnering a small crowd.

Hayley nudged him with her elbow. "You should get up there, show them your moves."

Okay, maybe there was a limit to what he would do in the name of love. "I knew introducing you to my sister would be a bad idea." He leaned down to kiss her. "She wants to know when she can meet you."

"Really? How's tomorrow for you?"

Harrison laughed. "I think I'm going to be busy tomorrow. In fact, I was thinking of sticking around for a few extra days. Maybe take a look around the city. Do you know anyone who might be interested in that?"

"If you're sticking around, you'll be lucky to see the outside of my bedroom."

"That a fact?" he asked against her lips.

"Mmm," she hummed into his mouth.

One year later...

51 EXT. CHANCE CITY - SHOWGROUNDS -
DAY

A sprawling crowd of people are
enjoying the Valentine's festival.
Harrison and Hayley walk hand in
hand along the stalls.

———

Hayley pulled on his hand, leaning up to kiss him on the cheek. "Stop looking so glum."

"I still can't believe I agreed to this."

"It's the fiftieth anniversary. We couldn't miss it."

"We could."

"Hush." She kissed him. "After last year, I thought you would enjoy being back."

"I enjoy being with you. I didn't imagine it would involve so many kissing booths," he said, gesturing to the one they passed. The line was impressive.

"There she is," Hayley said, pulling him toward an intricate floral showpiece. Two matching doves stood as tall as Harrison, their beaks touching, made of vibrant purple and red flowers. They were spectacular.

"Oh, Charlie, you've outdone yourself."

"Oh, hey, it's my inspiration!" Charlie said, hugging them both. "Get it? Lovebirds?"

"Still got that sense of humor," Harrison said.

"Still got that stick up your ass."

And okay, even he had to laugh at that.

"Stop checking your phone. Lee said we wouldn't hear back for a few days."

He knew that, but he couldn't help it. One of the best scripts he'd written in years — sorry, they'd written — had kicked off a bidding war. It was why they were here, on vacation, instead of at their apartment back home.

Harrison had been obsessively checking in for days, and Lee had stopped taking his calls.

Hayley kissed the corner of his mouth, slipping the phone out of his hands while he chased her lips. "Relax."

Up ahead was a small stage. Fairy lights were strung overhead, and a familiar musician was finishing up a song about a beach house. When the man spotted them approaching, he winked. "This one is for the lovers in the audience," he said before leading into the Nat King Cole song Harrison remembered so well.

He held his hand out. "Dance with me."

Hayley smiled, slipping her hand into his, the rock on her finger glittering in the daylight. He brought their hands to his lips, kissing the band.

"I have a new idea, and I want you to write it with me. It's about a world where there is no color, only beige." His smile widened at Hayley's fond eye roll. "And one day, two people cross paths and find that their meeting has introduced color into their lives."

"So it would be a modern-day *Pleasantville*?"

"You did say you wanted to work in adaptations," he said, kissing her cheek.

"Ah, so you do listen," she joked. "Does this mean" — she caught his mouth in a kiss — "that you want to write another romance?"

She tasted like sugar and tea. "I want to write my story."

This was it, he knew. Whatever happened, wherever they ended up, it would be together.

"See," Hayley said, swaying with him to the song. "I knew you were a romantic at heart."

FADE TO BLACK.

THE END

Thank you!

I can't thank you enough for reading my book! I hope you enjoyed reading it as much as I enjoyed writing it.

Want to share the love? Please consider leaving a review on Amazon, Goodreads, or even posting wherever you hang out online (BookTok, Bookstagram, Reddit). Comments and tags feed my romance reading soul.

I absolutely love to hear from my readers. What rom-com trope have you experienced in real life? Do you live for the Hallmark holiday movies as much as I do? (Even though everyone who has ever sat through these films knows I will make scathing commentary the entire time)

Message me anytime on any of my socials or contact me via contact@danimclean.com

Acknowledgments

To Hallmark, and every holiday themed Netflix movie for the tropes you celebrate. I don't always watch you without making fun of you, but it adds to the fun.

To Hollywood, for inspiring this book (and this entire series). My childhood was spent falling in love with films, and rom-coms will always hold a special place in my heart. And thank you for gifting us all the Chrises. We really appreciate it.

To all the screenwriters out there - you have the ability to give hope, joy, and love to your viewers - use that power wisely.

To Sam, the best cover designer in the world, who moves me with her art.

To Beth, the most patient person on the planet, thank you for putting up with me, and turning my words into books that I am not afraid to share with others.

To my bookstagram fam, you honestly do not know how much I appreciate you! You make social media a better place, and I love talking books with you all.

And to every single person who beta read, ARC read, commented, liked, shared, reviewed - THANK YOU.

About the Author

Dani McLean is an emerging author of Contemporary Romance stories that feature kickass women who can't quite get their shit together, and the irresistible but confused men who fall in love with them.

Born in Melbourne, she now lives in Perth, Western Australia with two walk in robes and a linen closet that's full of wine.

Dani loves to read, write and travel (in her memories, these days). She loves Hallmark movies because they're unintentionally hilarious, she's been on enough terrible Tinder dates to fuel countless books; and when she isn't conducting unofficial wine tastings in her pyjamas, she's devouring all things romance.

instagram.com/dmc_lean

facebook.com/danimcleanfiction

twitter.com/dmc_lean

tiktok.com/dmc_lean

amazon.com/author/danimclean

goodreads.com/danimclean

bookbub.com/authors/dani-mclean

Lightning Source UK Ltd.
Milton Keynes UK
UKHW040826021222
413139UK00008B/4